Western Wind

A Richard Jackson Book

. . . we spend our years as a tale that is told.

—Psalm 90:9

Western Wind

A NOVEL BY
Paula Fox

ORCHARD BOOKS / NEW YORK

Orchard Books
95 Madison Avenue
New York, NY 10016

Manufactured in the United States of America
Book design by Rosanne Kakos-Main
The text of this book is set in 14 point Perpetua.

10 9 8 7 6 5 4 3

Library of Congress Cataloging-in-Publication Data

Fox, Paula.
Western wind: a novel/by Paula Fox.
p.   cm.
Summary: Twelve-year-old Elizabeth resents being sent to stay
on a small Maine island after the arrival of her new baby
brother, but the time she spends with her artist grandmother
and an unusual young neighbor helps her to see things differently.
ISBN 0-531-06802-1. — ISBN 0-531-08652-6 (lib. bdg.)
[1. Grandmothers—Fiction. 2. Brothers and sisters—Fiction.
3. Islands—Fiction.] I. Title.
PZ7.F838We 1993 [Fic]—dc20
93-9629

T 19884

For Adam Burley

Six months after Elizabeth Benedict was born, her grandmother, Cora Ruth Benedict, moved to Maine. Now, eleven years later, Elizabeth was to spend the month of August with her on a small island in Penobscot Bay she had never seen, in a cottage without electricity or plumbing.

"What is there to do there? What will I *do*?" Elizabeth asked her father, Charles.

"There'll be plenty to do: swim—"

"Swim! I know about Maine swimming. You turn into a tray of ice cubes as soon as you stick your toe into that water," she said.

"The water is warmer in the coves," Daddy said.

"Coves!" exclaimed Elizabeth scornfully.

Daddy laughed. "That's the first time I ever heard *cove* used as a swear word."

"What about food? Or do we live off the land?" Elizabeth asked.

Daddy ignored her sarcastic tone. "There's a boat that comes to the island once a week from Molytown on the mainland. It'll bring groceries and mail—and we'll expect weekly letters from you."

"Groceries? Canned corn . . . stale bread," Elizabeth muttered.

"You have a poor attitude about this, my girl. You love Gran. Don't you? What's eating you?"

Elizabeth flushed and turned away. Love had nothing to do with it. She began to flip the pages of a law journal on a nearby table. Daddy knew what was eating her. She wasn't going to put into words what she felt—he would argue with her then, the way he probably did in court with a prosecutor.

She glanced at him over her shoulder. He was staring at her. She was startled by his expression, how uncertain he looked, as though he'd stumbled on evidence that didn't fit his case.

"I was going on the bicycle trip with Nancy to New Hampshire," she said. "I've been thinking about it for months."

She turned to face her father, feeling a faint hope she might still persuade him to go back to the original plan for August.

"The trip was only for a week. You can do that any summer. You're going to Gran, and that's that," he said matter-of-factly.

"Found guilty," Elizabeth said under her breath.

Her father smiled. She recognized the powerful grown-up smile of a parent who has made up his mind absolutely.

She started across the room to the door of the study.

"Where are you going?" he asked pleasantly.

"To pack winter clothes for August in Maine," she said as coolly as she dared.

OLD MRS. BENEDICT was not a grandmother in name only, as some of her friends' grandmothers were. Elizabeth, her father, her mother, Emilia, and Gran had visited each other as far back as she could remember. The younger Benedicts would go to Maine for a week or so as soon as Elizabeth's school closed for summer recess. They stayed in a bed-and-breakfast inn outside of Camden, where Gran had a small apartment overlooking a street that, she told Elizabeth, filled up with snow in winter and tourists in summer.

Ten years ago, Gran started renting the cottage on the island during July and August. It was a good place for a painter, she said. None of the Benedicts had visited her there. It was too hard to get to, Gran insisted, and it certainly wasn't big enough for four people. "We'd go mad!" she'd said.

"Why does she need two places at her age?" Elizabeth heard her father ask her mom. "In some ways, she's as extravagant as an adolescent."

"She's a painter," her mother had replied. "They never grow older than the age at which they began to paint."

It wasn't, Elizabeth knew, that her mother didn't care for her mother-in-law. But there was a kind of hesitation in her feeling for Gran, like a hiccup before you get out a word.

Elizabeth could hear that hesitation in the way her mother laughed, always a few seconds late, at something odd or comical Gran said. And she could see it when Gran came through the front door of their farmhouse north of Boston at Christmas, carrying her old morocco leather suitcase in one hand and a shopping bag of gifts in the other. Mom would nearly always wait a minute too long to hug her so that Gran, after a brief pause, would walk past her into the living room. Then she might say something like "I'm glad to see you haven't blocked up the fireplace yet" or "I hope you don't pull the shades down on these shorter days. The light is so smoky and mysterious. These folk around here tend to pull down their shades at five P.M., and they'll do it on the last day of the world."

Elizabeth could see her mother's mouth tighten at the very moment she was trying to smile.

The farmhouse had been Gran's before she'd deeded it over to Elizabeth's father and his family the year she'd moved north. Before that, before Elizabeth had been born, the three of them had lived together while Charles Benedict was finishing law school.

Even though Elizabeth's mother had already begun teaching the fifth grade in a local public school and had regular paychecks, living with

Gran had been a financial godsend, Daddy said. There hadn't been much money in those days.

Elizabeth understood how irritating Gran could be, yet she knew that her mother admired her. Elizabeth did, too. Though Gran didn't pay much attention to her as a rule, and she could be sharp.

One Thanksgiving, she'd told Elizabeth that if she described something as *cool* once more, she'd have her arrested for melting down the English language.

"The police don't arrest you for that," Elizabeth responded.

"I'll make a citizen's arrest," said Gran, and burst into laughter.

That was how it often went between the young Benedicts and the old Benedict. Gran would say something cutting, then smile or laugh outright. But when she was around, there was an edge to the days, a kind of nervy liveliness. Even Elizabeth's father, a rather silent man, would grow talkative, arguing with Gran about painters he thought were better than she did, or about the government, which he thought worse than she did, and about a dozen other things. The hundred-year-old conversation, Elizabeth called it in her mind.

Now and then, on a rainy day, Elizabeth would go up to the attic that Gran had used for a studio when she had lived in the farmhouse. There were two old steamer trunks there, a battered easel near the big north-facing window, and a few canvasses propped against an unfinished wall. Some pencil sketches were still tacked to a rickety screen. One was of Elizabeth as a tiny infant. At times she thought it looked like her, but at other times it could have been any infant in the world.

There was one finished painting among the canvasses. It was a winter landscape. Two crows sat on a fence that slanted across snow-covered corn stubble in a long field that reached to the horizon. Elizabeth liked that painting and told Gran so.

"It looks just like what I see out the window in winter," she'd said.

"Do you only like what you can recognize?" Gran asked her. She seemed really curious.

"How can I like something I can't recognize?" Elizabeth asked after thinking a moment.

"Why do you have to like everything?" Gran asked.

Elizabeth was speechless.

"I mean," Gran went on in an unusually gentle voice, "can't you just be interested in things? And forget about liking?"

She'd brought Elizabeth a small pearl ring one Christmas. She'd found it in a shop on a shabby boulevard in Paris.

"One of those places you can't imagine surviving from one week to another, like some of the little stores you see here in town. The owner had a few rings in the window, a cameo or two, a boring gold chain, and the ring I got you. The shop was no bigger than a closet, but when I went inside I saw that the walls were covered with photographs of a beautiful chestnut racehorse. It turned out the man owned that horse. It had won two races for him. Suzerain was its name, and it was what he most loved in the world. He kept the shop to support the horse, not himself. I found out he was originally from Algiers. Your little ring is connected to all of that, Elizabeth. Do you know where Algiers is?"

"Sort of," Elizabeth had replied.

"'Sort of' won't do for geography," Gran said. So very soon, she'd found an atlas in the house and shown Elizabeth just where Algiers was, and told her a few things about colonies and revolutions.

Gran was an encyclopedia of her own interests.

But she didn't know much about music of any kind. As for books, all Gran read was poetry, or the diaries and letters of painters. She could see why people liked stories, she told Elizabeth, but after a few pages of a novel, she'd find herself dropping the book and going to a window or a door to look out at something, a bird winging its way across the sky, or a tree branch, or even some tourist on the street below her living-room window in Camden, pausing a moment to stare around blankly and scratch his bottom.

What poetry told her, Gran said, was "about the hidden and true life inside yourself," about longing and hope and sorrow. In that conversation, Elizabeth had felt oppressed by Gran's words, her intent expression. She'd felt a powerful impulse to shout something rude.

Once, Gran had read to her a few letters a painter named Vincent van Gogh had written to his brother, Theo. It seemed to Elizabeth that they were all about not having any money and needing to buy paints.

"What do you think?" Gran had asked her when she'd finished reading. "Did you notice that he didn't even mention he was half-starved?"

Elizabeth didn't know what she thought. But she felt a small thrill of pleasure, as she always did when Gran spoke to her that way—as if she could think if only she would.

During these exchanges, Elizabeth didn't feel Gran was paying attention to her so much as she was paying attention to what most concerned her. She never asked Elizabeth about schoolwork or grades, or what she wanted to be when she grew up. Elizabeth had to admit to herself that it was a relief that she didn't.

Yet despite all the things about Gran that made her fun to be with, unpredictable and ungrandmotherly, she was the last person on earth Elizabeth wanted to spend a whole month with.

She knew exactly why she was being sent away. It was because of Stephen Lindsay Benedict, one week old on July 19, her brother, around whose bassinet her parents stood as though it held a holy object, and whose raspy kitten cries woke Elizabeth all night long.

Mom and Daddy were old, in their forties. What kind of a thing to do was that—at their age? By the time the baby was as old as Elizabeth, they'd be using walkers.

"We didn't really plan him," Mom said to Elizabeth, her face rosy and smiling. Elizabeth shuddered. "But that's life," Mom said, as she pressed the wrapped-up bundle with the red moony face close to her chest.

When Elizabeth first told her friend Nancy that her mother was going to have a baby, she was embarrassed. She could barely get the words out.

Nancy looked grave. "And they call us irresponsible," she remarked.

"It's disgusting," Elizabeth burst out, and felt a twinge of guilt.

The worst part of it, now that Stephen Lindsay had arrived to live in the old farmhouse, was a thing she couldn't bear to say out loud. It was that her parents wanted to be alone with the little thing so much that they could hardly wait to get her out of the house.

Then they could eat him all up. Pet him and spoil him. Murmur and croon and smile foolishly while he split the walls with his howls for attention.

⊰2⊱

Elizabeth flew from Boston to Bangor, Maine. It was the first time she had been on an airplane. She sat next to the small, scratched window, looking down on the earth below. Much of the land seemed arranged in patterns so precise they might have been drawn with a ruler. "It will look sort of cubist from up there," Gran had told her on the telephone when she spoke with Elizabeth about arrangements to meet her. "You'll find it a different view. . . ."

Last summer, Gran had had a show of her work at a Camden gallery. Despite Elizabeth's faint discomfort at being introduced as the artist's granddaughter, she'd been pleased, too. Gran was wearing small turquoise earrings and a long clay-colored linen skirt and shirt when

15

she arrived at the gallery. She had looked pretty good. But Elizabeth didn't like her new paintings, about which Gran had also said to her, "sort of cubist."

Fortunately, Gran never appeared to expect her to make comments about her work.

As the plane began its descent to Bangor, Elizabeth felt a kind of anticipation she couldn't account for. She was still resentful that her parents, Mom carrying Stephen Lindsay, ridiculous in a sun hat that made him look like a cream puff, had left her much too quickly at the airport gate.

Gran was waiting for her at the gate. She hugged her briefly, held her arm by the wrist, looked at her steadily for a minute, and said, "Let's get your stuff and get out of here."

They drove for over two hours, the road following the Penobscot River part of the way, until they arrived at a small settlement, Molytown, whose narrow wooden housefronts, like the faces of old, quiet people, overlooked Penobscot Bay.

Gran parked her dusty, noisy old car in a roughly carpentered garage, where it would stay for the month, near an open shed filled with stacks of lobster pots. She'd gone on and on about the car during most of the drive— how it had cost only three hundred dollars, how Ray, a local mechanic, had done a lovely job fixing it up, how salt air affected cars. Elizabeth had been silent.

Now, as she stood waiting while Gran locked up the car, she sniffed the air. It had a prickling, lively smell, different from the dampish country air at home that she was used to in August. She was suddenly eager to go out onto that vast bay that was like a tray holding bits of land on its metal blue surface.

"We have to call your father and tell him you arrived safely," Gran said. "I'll pick up a few things at the store." She pointed down the street that ran past several long wharves standing on tall spider legs, to a small store that bore a sign: SADIE'S FOOD. "There's a public telephone just outside. Would you like to make the call?"

Elizabeth shook her head. She tried to smile, aware of how long she had been silent. Gran shrugged and went off along the street, and Elizabeth sat down on a wooden crate near the shed.

She was actually in Maine with Gran. She realized that she'd been hoping for a reprieve at the last moment, even as her parents had said good-bye to her in Boston. It seemed to her, now, that the bicycle she had so often imagined herself pedaling through New Hampshire villages had rolled away on its own to collapse in a corner of the farmhouse cellar. Yet there was another feeling, strong and insistent, that— despite herself—she was about to be happy.

Gran appeared soon, carrying a paper sack.

"Your daddy says hello and love," she reported. "There's our transportation." She waved at the nearest wharf, where Elizabeth saw a small boat bobbing at the end of a long rope tied to a piling.

"We're going in that?" exclaimed Elizabeth. "It's like a pea pod!"

"We're going in that," Gran said brusquely.

They walked out on the wharf, which swayed and creaked beneath their feet. Gran pulled on the rope until the boat was close to a ladder that descended into the water. "It's easier when the tide isn't so low," Gran said.

Along the bottom of the boat lay a pair of oars, a rolled tarpaulin, and rags. To Elizabeth's relief, a small outboard motor clung like a claw to the stern.

"I'll go first. Then you start down and hand me your suitcase and backpack and the groceries," Gran said, descending the ladder with sure steps.

Elizabeth handed down the things and stepped into the rocking boat herself. "Do you have to cross over from the island every time you need something from the store?" she asked.

"Oh, no! I'd be at sea all the time. See the launch over there? The one with *El Sueño* written on the bow? That's Jake Holborn's. He brings it over to Pring Island once a week. I give him a list. Next time, he brings me what I asked for, and the mail. The launch was built seventy years ago. It used to carry servants and supplies out to the rich people who once owned many of the islands in the bay. It's a beautiful old thing, isn't it? Like my car. Jake keeps the brass polished."

A gull flew to one of the pilings and folded its wings. It seemed to stare coldly at Elizabeth.

"But what if you need something in a hurry? Do you have a phone?"

"Put the stuff in front of you, Elizabeth, and sit in the middle of the seat. We don't need a phone. There is a family on the island, the Herkimers."

The motor roared, then settled down to a modest grumble. The boat nosed its way past the wharf. Elizabeth was preoccupied with the news that there were other people on the island. She didn't even glance up when Gran announced they were passing *El Sueño*.

"John Herkimer has a battery-run shortwave radio. And Jake has a receiver on the launch, so we can reach him when he's on it, which is most of the time. When there are storms, John's radio doesn't fail like a telephone might. It's the same for electricity and water. The hand pump in the cottage works no matter what the weather is doing. And as long as we have matches, we can keep the kerosene lamps or candles lit."

Gran put on a scarf and tied it with one hand, her other on the tiller. Elizabeth's dark straight hair was blown into tangles by a low, brisk breeze. She saw islands everywhere. Some were quilled like porcupines with evergreen trees.

Some were large jagged rocks stained with pale green lichen. As they passed one such tumbled, stony place, Elizabeth cried out, "There's a seal!"

"They like to sun themselves," Gran shouted over the sound of the motor, which had grown loud now that they were out on the bay, away from Molytown's sheltering harbor. "And that's where I found Grace, my cat."

"How did a cat get there?"

"She'd been abandoned. Someone must have put her off a boat. She was dehydrated and terrified but managed to scramble into my lap. I had to grab on to barnacles to keep the boat steady while she slid down. Fortunately, it was high tide."

"How could anyone do such an awful thing?" Elizabeth stared at the rocks, trying to imagine the people who could have left a small animal in such a desolate place. What had they thought?

"I don't know," Gran answered. "I tend to believe in demons. Other explanations for such behavior seem wanting."

The boat had changed direction. They were heading straight for a heavily wooded island.

"That's Pring," Gran said.

As Elizabeth stared, the island appeared slowly to emerge from the bay. An uneven ridge along the center of it suggested the menacing rise and fall of a dinosaur spine. Between the ranks of pine, glimpses of sky were like silent explosions of brilliant blue.

Gran cut the motor speed, and they moved slowly past a stone-strewn beach. Beyond it lay a sloping meadow of tall, tawny grass.

Elizabeth dipped her hand in the water and withdrew it quickly. It was like ice.

Gran glanced at her. "A person can't last more than two minutes out here," she said. "But closer to shore, in the coves, the sun warms up the water and you can swim if you can bear it."

At the foot of the ridge, Elizabeth saw a large, rambling house. Near it stood a small barn, its roof collapsed, tendrils of vine wound thickly around the walls. Here and there, great patches of bramble sat bristling like indignant fowl.

"Is that your house?" Elizabeth asked.

"It's the Herkimer place. He's a high-school teacher in Orono. She runs the local historical society there. The family has been coming here for twenty years. We're going to have supper with them tomorrow. Hold on now."

They rounded a point of land that was no more than a splinter of coarse sand and pebbles. At once, they were in a small cove, and the Herkimer house was hidden by a slight rise, upon which stood clumps of oak and pine. Gran brought the boat to a dock, tied up next to a ladder, and said, "Pring." She smiled at Elizabeth, who was staring at a shell path that led to the door of a ramshackle, dark little cottage.

"That's your house?" Elizabeth asked, unable to conceal the disappointment she felt.

"That's it," Gran said shortly, her smile gone. "Begin unloading, please."

After Elizabeth had transferred everything to the dock, Gran unrolled the tarp and spread it over the boat. The journey was done. Pring was a piece of earth covered with stones and rocks and scraggly trees. The cottage had a dull, blank look.

Mom and Daddy were playing with Stephen Lindsay at home. On the marble-topped kitchen table, there was probably a big bag of fresh corn and warm tomatoes from the farm stand down the road. Elizabeth looked inside Gran's grocery sack. She saw a carton of milk and a can of navy beans.

Gran came to stand beside her. "It will be twilight soon. I like that time of day best. And very early morning," she said. "Tomorrow, you can explore the other shore of the island. It's quite different from this side."

She was standing so close! Elizabeth stared down at the splintery surface of the dock.

"You don't much want to be here," Gran stated. "I know that."

Elizabeth looked up, but away from her grandmother. A small bird flew toward the squat oak trees on the rise.

"We'll make the best of it," Gran said. "That means we have to find something more interesting to think about than your disappointment at being here."

"I'm not disappointed," Elizabeth protested weakly. "It's just that I'm not used to islands —the water. Anyhow, you don't have to think about it."

"Never mind all that," Gran retorted sharply. "Life is all getting used to what you're not used to."

Then she smiled. "Look! There's Grace!"

From a side of the cottage, a small smoke gray cat walked toward them, her tail straight up like an exclamation point.

⚛3⚛

Inside the cottage, there were not three or four tight, dark rooms as Elizabeth had imagined, but one big room. Two rows of four wooden posts, about a dozen feet apart, rose to the ceiling. They were like the columns of a small temple. At the base of one, she deposited the luggage and groceries and looked around.

Next to a sink beneath a window stood a stumpy hand pump on a counter. Beside it were two glasses, one with a toothbrush, the other filled with Queen Anne's lace. Shelves above and below the counter held dishes, glasses, pots, pans, and canned food. Along the same wall hulked a big wood stove; a few feet away stood a small two-door chest. On the floor were bottles and baskets filled with flowers, some fresh, some dried. A stack of wood lay next to the dark hearth of a tiny fireplace.

There were several chairs, a round table, and next to other windows across the room from the sink, an easel splotched with paint. A wide plank on two sawhorses held cans of brushes, sticks of charcoal, tubes of paint, a palette, and a Polaroid camera. A small staircase, with a handrail made of rope, disappeared into shadows.

The room was inviting without looking very comfortable. It appeared to have no secrets— like a person who tells you right away what she's interested in. Yet some mystery remained. Perhaps it was because of the posts that were like temple columns, or because of the implements and materials of painting that covered the wide plank.

Grace sped past Elizabeth, leaped on a ragged red sweater on the floor near the easel, and began to scratch one ear.

"Sand fleas," observed Gran, who had come to the door.

"Where shall I put the groceries?"

"On the counter. Put the milk in the icebox."

"The icebox?" Elizabeth asked politely, knowing it was the little chest.

Gran was silent.

Chagrined, Elizabeth opened the bottom door of the icebox and thrust the milk inside. A watery smell, edged with sourness, emanated from its dark interior. There was food on a shelf, but Elizabeth didn't try to make out what it was.

"What do you think?" Gran asked.

"About what?"

"Well—I hoped you would have a thought about this place," Gran said.

"It doesn't look like your apartment in Camden."

"No, it doesn't."

"It's really pretty there," Elizabeth said, knowing how disagreeable she was being, unable to stop herself.

"I suppose it is," Gran said pleasantly.

Elizabeth clamped her jaw shut and stared down at her old running shoes. How ugly they were! Carelessly tied, dirty, big as boats. She would have gotten new ones for the bicycle trip.

"I'm so sorry you feel the way you seem to," Gran said softly.

Elizabeth's throat tightened. Her eyes swam with sudden tears. She swallowed hard and looked over at Gran.

"Walk around a bit," Gran urged. "It'll lighten your heart." She went to the counter and began to put away the food she'd bought at Sadie's.

Elizabeth wandered toward the easel. She noticed that there were paintings hung on all the walls of the room. Some were washes of color. Others were recognizable—woods, the ridge that ran along the center of the island, rocks. Sketches of Grace covered a sheet of paper. One big canvas showed a group of people who looked like a family posing for a photographer on some special occasion. Everywhere, in oil or ink or charcoal, were drawings and paintings of a man's head. Some were a few lines. Others were detailed. In one, a hat brim hid the man's forehead and eyes so that only his falconlike nose and long narrow mouth showed.

"The good thing is I don't have to clean very often," Gran said. Elizabeth turned around and saw she was standing at the foot of the stairs.

"Come and see your room," Gran said.

"Were there once lots of little rooms here?"

"Yes. I got a carpenter from Molytown to take down the walls after the owner said I could do whatever I wanted to. It was too dark before, too squeezed. The posts hold up the ceiling so he had to leave them. I like them, though."

Elizabeth, carrying her bag and pack, followed Gran up the stairs to a small landing.

Gran opened one of the two doors that led off it. "I'd thought you'd like to be able to see the bay," she said.

The room ran the width of the house. A braided rug lay on the floor beside an iron bed-stead that was covered with a blue and red quilt. Next to it stood a night table holding a candle in a saucer. Another candle and a jar full of wildflowers stood on the bureau. A small mirror in a hammered-tin frame hung from a nail on the wall above a straight-backed chair with a towel folded on it.

"I put some hangers here on the back of the door, if you have anything you need to hang," Gran said.

Elizabeth thought of the two summer dresses she'd packed. No use for them here.

"Can I wash my face and hands?" she asked.

"At the sink," Gran answered. "There's very good water on Pring. Some of the islands have none; that's why they're uninhabitable. I'll show you the facilities after you've unpacked. You'll have to take sponge baths. That's what you had when you were a baby. In fact, I gave you a few of those myself. You can heat water on the stove when you need it."

Elizabeth unzipped her bag. When she looked up, Gran was gone. She walked to one of two small windows so close to the floor she had to stoop to see out. The mainland seemed much farther away than her sense of the distance she and Gran had traveled in the little boat.

Below, she saw the clamshell path leading to the dock, alongside of which the boat rocked gently. The waters of the bay were as purple now as a Concord grape. The tide had risen and covered the small point of land that made one arm of the cove.

With some difficulty, Elizabeth pushed up the creaking window and stuck her head outside. The air was pungent with the smell of pine and salt. Across the sky to the west, she saw streaks of red as thin as paper cuts. A gull shrieked. She watched it swoop to the dock, where it cradled itself in its wings and became as still as stone. There was such silence! She couldn't hear Gran below. Water and sky seemed one joined, immense thing in which she floated, a speck.

There was a thud, a loud meow, and she turned to see Grace standing on the red and blue quilt, switching her tail and looking at her.

Elizabeth sighed, stroked the cat a minute, and began to put away her clothes. On the bedside table, she put two novels from her school's summer reading list, *To Kill a Mockingbird* and *The Old Man and the Sea*, neither of which she had yet glanced at. How could she have read in a house where everybody was waiting for a baby to wake up, or else running around like crazed mice when he did?

She took the towel from the chair and her toothbrush and went down the stairs.

Gran was peering into the upper part of the icebox. "It's a good thing Jake's coming day after tomorrow. The ice is nearly gone," she said. "It only lasts about five days. I hope you like spaghetti. I've made tomato sauce. And I picked blueberries this morning before I went to Bangor. You'll be sick of blueberries before you leave Pring. Put your toothbrush in the glass next to the pump. I'll show you the outhouse."

Elizabeth followed Gran to the back of the cottage and up the rise. There, in a fragrant thicket of young spruce, stood a small outhouse, entirely open on the side that faced the bay. Leaves of thick ivy framed it.

"It doesn't have a door," Elizabeth said.

"A door wouldn't make it more private out here, just stuffy," Gran said. "I've seen deer close by in the early morning," she added.

"How would a deer get here?"

"Swim. I once saw one swimming. Very beautiful, holding its head well above the water, like

35

a creature from a fairy tale. Fire can drive them out of the forests on the mainland, or hunger."

When they returned to the cottage, Gran talked about the Herkimers as she led Elizabeth by her hand to the large painting of the family she had noticed earlier. "There they are. The whole gang," Gran said.

Two older people in bathing suits looked grimly out of the painting. A girl of around fourteen stood on one leg, holding the other bent sideways with a long-fingered hand. She wore an old-fashioned party dress, bright pink and covered with bows. Kneeling in front was a little boy with large transparent ears and huge eyes as dark as coal. The woman's right hand rested above his head, not touching it. Far in the background stood the long house and collapsed barn.

"John and Helen Herkimer," said Gran. "The girl, Deirdre, would never put on such a dress. She was wearing torn blue jeans when she posed for me. My little joke. The boy is Aaron. He's a strange child. His ears aren't actually like the ones I painted. It's that he listens so intently you feel he's *all* ears. His parents are awfully nervous about him. Helen watches him all the time. Usually, he spends the summer with her brother, but the brother had a stroke this spring. So Aaron's here for the first time."

"What makes them so nervous?"

"I don't know. Aaron can't get lost on this island, and the water temperature doesn't encourage impulsive swimming. But it's true he doesn't seem to understand danger. He climbed up on their roof last week. They had a frightening time getting him down in one piece."

"Funny, to wear such a lot of pearls with a bathing suit," commented Elizabeth.

"Helen always wears them. Years ago, her first husband ran away from her. I heard from people in Camden who've known her for years that she never got over feeling disgraced. It's said that when she found the note he left, she put on the pearls and has never taken them off, even in the hospital when the children were born. The family is really like a small country. Maybe all proper families are. I feel I need a passport to visit them. Occasionally, I think they're going to revoke my visa. If I wasn't their only neighbor, I do believe they'd have nothing to do with me. Helen is very disdainful. When I take a walk in the early evening and pass their house, I sometimes hear her laughing, and I know she's making fun of someone, probably me."

"They don't sound so great."

"I like them, though. Maybe *like* isn't quite the word."

"Maybe you're interested in them," said Elizabeth, with a slight emphasis, recalling how Gran had asked her if she had to like everything.

"Ah! That must be it," Gran said with amusement. She was rolling up newspaper sheets and thrusting them into the wood stove. As Gran added kindling, Elizabeth picked up the Polaroid camera and looked through its viewfinder at the room. There was a yellow glow at the west-facing windows.

"Take a look at those birds out on the sand spit," Gran suggested. "Every afternoon, even when it's foggy, they come to sit there and look toward the sunset. Some kind of bird religion."

The fire caught, and soon Gran had filled a large, dented pot with water from the pump and placed it on one of the stove lids, around which Elizabeth saw a red rim like a corona. After that, she washed lettuce leaves, one by one.

"You don't mind bottled dressing, do you? I'm too old for vinaigrette. I'll light the lamps now."

Soon the room was awash in a pale yellow glow from several kerosene lamps. Now the posts were like trees that had grown inside the cottage.

A vivid memory came to Elizabeth. She was sitting at the kitchen table at home while Mom sorted clothes that had dried in the sun that afternoon. Elizabeth was crayoning. She recalled the feel of the thick, waxy crayons, the rough surface of the drawing paper in front of her, the radio on low, playing piano music, evening coming softly across the fields like smoke. She had felt so safe.

She put the camera back on the plank table. "It's very quiet here," she said.

"I have a small battery radio I get the weather on. You can play it, if you like."

Gran, busy at the stove, didn't see her shake her head no. Elizabeth drifted toward the staircase to look at some snapshots tacked to the wall there.

Surprised, she said, "These pictures are all of the cottage."

"When I visit painter friends of mine," Gran said, "and I see their big, well-lit studios, I get envious. Then, when I come back here in July, everything looks shabby and dark. A mess! So I took those snaps. They seem to let me see the place in a different way. I remember why I loved it the first time I saw it."

"You have the apartment in Camden."

"I don't feel much about that place. It's comfortable, but sort of elderly."

Didn't Gran know she was old?

"But you couldn't live here in winter," Elizabeth said. "It'd be so cold."

"And lonely," remarked Gran. "No, I couldn't. Not anymore. . . . Your grandfather and I once lived on a mountain in New Mexico where your face froze when you opened the door. Our cabin was not even half the size of this place. We kept warm in front of a potbellied stove, and cooked on it, too. We stuck it out for two months."

She dropped strands of thin spaghetti into the dented pot, now rocking in place as the water boiled furiously.

Elizabeth's grandfather had died long before she was born. He'd only been a word, a name for a blank space.

"William, always called Will," Gran said, turning to smile at her. "You're tall and thin the way he was. That's him in all those sketches on the wall. Did you know he was a lawyer, too, like your father? We wandered around for a few years; then he was called up for the army during World War Two. He was in the South Pacific three years. When he came back, he went to law school with government help. Before that—well, anything seemed possible. You could live on very little. You could almost invent your life as you went along. I had started to paint, and Will wanted to be a poet. That cabin we rented for a few dollars a month probably costs a million today. When he came back from the army—I remember the very moment he said it—he told me loving poetry wasn't enough. He didn't have it in him. But he became a very good lawyer."

Elizabeth suddenly recalled that her mother had told her she had to be more helpful around the house than she was at home, that Gran tired much more easily than she let on.

"Shall I set the table?" she asked.

"Put out two dishes and forks and spoons," Gran said. "We're out of bread. Jake will bring it the day after tomorrow. I hope you won't mind crackers and oranges for breakfast."

The spaghetti was good, the bottled dressing not bad, the blueberries fresh and sweet. While they ate, Gran told her stories about living in New Mexico.

Elizabeth sensed that Gran wasn't recollecting things only to amuse her. She kept a steady gaze on Elizabeth's face as she spoke, the way people do when they are serious and want you to remember what they are telling you.

"One evening, a big truck full of Arkansas families parked near our cabin. They were sawyers—woodcutters—and they'd been timbered out, no more trees to cut. Four families looking for work, children, even an old dog, all sliding off the tailgate. We gave them water and some boxes of Fig Newtons we kept around. They invited us to breakfast next morning. We had to get up at four A.M. They wanted an early start. When the sun rose, it looked no brighter than the big fire they made. I've never had such a breakfast. Biscuits made in a frying pan, bacon and eggs and grits. Later, they drove off, banging and rattling on the rough road, the children dangling their legs over the end of the truck and the old dog trying to curl itself into a lie-down position. I think it was the first time Will and I realized there was a river of people moving around the country, looking for work. People are out of work again now, and moving. But I doubt they start their days with such good breakfasts. Would you mind filling up the big pot with water and putting it on the stove? While it's heating, we can go out and look at the sky. You'll have to heat water to wash your clothes as well as dishes."

Elizabeth hadn't washed clothes before, just dropped them into the washing machine. She did remember that when she was little, she'd destroyed a doll's party dress when she soaked it in liquid floor polish she'd thought was soap.

They walked out of the cottage and toward the dock.

"New moon rising," Gran said. "'Sky canoe,' Wordsworth called it."

There was a tremor of light on the water, like a silver needle writing something undecipherable. Above the dark mass of land in the distance, Elizabeth saw the moon. It did look like a canoe made of light. She heard the mumble of water on the shore, withdrawing, returning. An eerie cry pierced the silence.

"Loon," Gran whispered. She was standing next to Elizabeth, her hands clasped. "I've never wanted anyone tramping around my cottage," she said. "But I'm glad you're here."

I was sent away——Elizabeth's inner voice spoke its refrain fiercely——*sent away, sent away.* . . . Gran's words didn't warm her. They frightened her, made her uncertain about her own explanation to herself of why she was on this island. If it hadn't been Stephen Lindsay's birth, then what had it been?

To her further dismay, Gran began to recite a poem.

"Western wind, when wilt thou blow,
The small rain down can rain?
Christ, if my love were in my arms
And I in my bed again!

"No one knows who wrote that," Gran said. "It's called 'Absence' and it's over four hundred years old. Will liked it."

Hurriedly, Elizabeth asked, "What happens out here in a really bad storm?"

Gran walked back to the cottage, and Elizabeth followed, ashamed of herself and angry that she felt so. She bent to pet Grace, who had followed them outside and was now winding about her ankles. But as soon as she touched the cat, Grace sped away.

"You wish I hadn't told you the poem," Gran stated.

"No. I just—"

"Go inside. I have to shut the door. If the wind shifts, we'll get mosquitoes."

The room seemed much lighter since they'd been outdoors.

Gran walked to the stove to pour the hot water into a basin. "During the night, I have to make several trips to the outhouse. I hope I won't wake you. There's a flashlight in your bureau in case you have to go. Watch out for tree roots."

"I'll be careful," Elizabeth said, wanting only to be in her room with the door shut.

Gran washed the supper dishes, rinsing them in a pan of cold water.

After a while, without looking at Elizabeth, she said in a stern voice, "That poem has lasted because it has such truth of feeling, of longing, in it."

"I was embarrassed!" Elizabeth burst out.

At once, Gran turned around. She smiled. "You'll have to get used to me saying a poem now and then. I swear to you, you're not obliged to listen. It's a habit I got from Will."

Elizabeth didn't know what to say, but it was as though a dreadful knot in her stomach had suddenly untied itself.

"I'll go to the outhouse now," she said. "There aren't any snakes, are there?"

"No big ones. Just little nervous things that'll wriggle away when they hear you."

She didn't need a flashlight to find her way. The sky was luminous. A faint wind had risen. Around the outhouse, the ivy leaves rustled. The lights Elizabeth saw seemed very far away, flickering like earthbound stars. They probably came from Molytown or from a boat anchored out on the bay.

When she returned to the cottage, only a single lamp was lit.

"Bring up the lamp," Gran called from the upstairs. "In the morning, you can take it down again."

In her room, Elizabeth placed the lamp on the bedside table. She put on her pajamas and went to kneel at the window.

Mom and Daddy could not have known how Gran lived on Pring, how the most ordinary things you never thought about—washing a dish, going to the bathroom—had to be learned in this place.

She thought of how she had watched her parents from the airplane. They had paused, she remembered now, probably trying to spot her through one of the windows in the long slope of the plane.

She had realized briefly, before the plane began to slide away from the loading platform, that they were having an argument. She knew how they'd sound, Daddy pretending he was trying to calm a maniac, Mom getting more and more stirred up because she knew Daddy's reasonableness was fake. Then she saw Stephen Lindsay rear back and open his mouth. Her parents had both clutched at him. If she thought of it as a silent movie, it was pretty funny.

Suddenly, as she stared through the small window, she saw four figures come around the sand spit and walk slowly toward Gran's dock. They appeared cloaked, sinister. Then a small figure broke away from the group and began to dance ahead, leaping from side to side.

At once, the two larger figures ran after the dancer, waving their arms about.

"Aaron!" Elizabeth heard a woman's voice cry out. "Aaron! Come back here at once!"

⚜ 4 ⚜

In the morning, the light was dull and gray. Through the window, Elizabeth saw Gran standing on the path below, holding a mug in one hand. Grace sat on a patch of grass close beside her. She guessed that Gran and her cat started every day like that. They looked lonesome.

She dressed, yawning. She had slept like a stone sunk in the sea. As she passed Gran's room, she glanced in. It had a severe appearance, as though it would refuse to contain more than was already in it: narrow bed, chair, table, a small, cloudy mirror above a small chest of drawers.

Downstairs, Gran was skinning an orange and dividing it into sections. A dish of saltines sat upon the round table.

"Good morning, Elizabeth. There's some warm water in the pan to wash up with."

"Good morning. I'll go out to the bathroom first."

When she returned, the radio was playing softly on the floor next to Gran's easel.

"When you've finished breakfast, you might want to look around," Gran said. "Go up behind the outhouse and you'll find a path that will lead you over the ridge to the other shore. It's wilder there. There's only one island beyond Pring and no one lives on it. The tides wash up odd things. Once I found a quite good wood carving of a rhinoceros. Strange object to find on a Maine beach. I used to gather blue mussels there on the rocks, but I slip and slide too much these days. If you want to collect some, we can steam them for lunch."

Elizabeth nodded and ate her crackers and orange.

"Do you mind if I take some snapshots of you?" Gran asked. Elizabeth looked down at her torn jeans. "It's not for beauty," Gran said. "I use the snaps for drawing."

Elizabeth shrugged. For the first time, she used the hand pump, intending to heat water to wash her dish. The rush of bluish water was immensely satisfying.

"Just brush the crumbs off the plate," Gran said. "We can do without a few amenities here."

Elizabeth heard the buzzing of the Polaroid. She was used to the sound. As long as she could recall, her parents had taken pictures of her. Now they would be doing the same with Stephen Lindsay, making faces and silly noises so he'd liven up for the camera. She thought of her own infant pictures. You might as well take shots of a banana in a dish.

"I'm going to work. Morning is the good time for me. My energy tends to run out like the tide as the day goes on."

A ray of sunlight touched the old planks of the floor.

Gran held out her hand as though to touch the warmth. "Good," she murmured.

"I'll take a walk," Elizabeth said.

Gran smiled vaguely, looking at her work-table.

As Elizabeth passed the outhouse, a breeze sprang up, and by the time she had emerged from the trees, the sun had cleared away the morning haze.

She found the path, narrow as a snake, faint as a tracing, leading across the glossy leaves of some kind of ground cover. It went part of the way up the ridge and petered out among rocks and sandy earth where stunted trees grew no higher than her knees. From the crest, she looked down upon a scene in which there seemed no place for humans to walk, to rest, on that turbulent edge of land, gleaming wetly, its several half-hidden coves ringing as waves broke in them. Pinkish-colored boulders pressed against the ridge as if backing away from the sea. Dark, jagged rocks rose up like stone geysers. What beach there was, was covered with stones and patches of coarse sand or thick tufts of swordlike grass. Everywhere, flung by the tides, were pieces of driftwood.

Elizabeth wiped the sweat from her face and began the descent. Once she slid and held on, gasping, to the hard-packed earth. At her back, the wind pressed like a great flat hand. Her hair hung in her eyes, tickled her mouth. At last, she came to rest on a huge rock shaped like a saucer.

She braided her hair and looked out to sea, where birds swooped and rose like torn strips of paper. She felt buoyant as the wind blew against her, and even, it seemed, through her. They had sent her away . . . and she didn't care.

She wished there were a long beach; she would have run for hours. As it was, she had to pick her way among the stones. She paused in a cove to stare at a dense colony of mussels clinging to a rock, around which purplish weeds floated. She shuddered at the thought of eating them. When she bent to feel the water, her hand acted like a siphon, drawing up the coldness until she felt it in her bones. It might have been minutes or hours that she wandered along that shore. When she had decided she'd had enough of it, she found an easier slope leading up to the crest of the ridge. The lee side looked calm and tame. On the bay, she saw several small boats that would pause, move quickly on, then pause again—lobster boats, probably— and one sailboat, its canvas billowing. As she descended, the wind dropped and she felt the full heat of the sun.

Below her was the roof of the Herkimer house and the collapsed barn. As she looked down, wondering about the people who lived in the place, the boy, Aaron, came running out of a door and hurled a vermilion Frisbee into the air.

"There's my own moon!" he shouted so loudly Elizabeth heard each word.

In a few seconds, a girl ran toward him and grabbed him. They struggled briefly until she pinned him to the ground. He lay still like a small, toppled statue. The girl sat up. Aaron, as though electrified, sprang to his feet and raced back into the house. At that moment, the girl looked up, spotted Elizabeth, and stuck her thumbs in her ears and waggled her fingers.

When Elizabeth got back to the cottage, Gran was bending over a cabinet. "Hell is trying to get a big frying pan onto a crowded pot-and-pan shelf," she said. "Did you see the sea? You've been gone for hours. Oh! Your face is so red! I should have given you something to put on. It's hard to keep in mind all the new warnings."

Did Gran talk to herself when nobody was around? Elizabeth wondered.

"I saw Aaron," she said. "He ran out of the house and his sister came right after him. Last night, I saw them, too, all walking toward your dock. He jumped a few feet ahead of them, and they acted as if he were going to run across the water to Molytown."

"He does like to startle them. I heard he once got into their car when he was five or so and managed to start it and drive several blocks before they caught him."

Now that it was noon and the sun was overhead, it was darker in the room. Gran was pushing her easel closer to the window.

"When you're old," she said, "what you want is light. Your eyes change. You begin to see much more yellow in everything. That presents an interesting problem to painters. About lunch—there's peanut butter and jelly and some tomatoes. We have the milk we got yesterday."

Yesterday! It seemed a week ago!

"I saw a lot of driftwood on the other shore," Elizabeth said. "You must have some storms out here."

"We do. Grace and I have sat in the middle of this room waiting to be blown to Oz like Dorothy and Toto. Nature's violence doesn't leave you much time to be scared. Human violence is something else." She began to clean a brush. "I was staying with a friend in Texas once," she went on, "when a hurricane hit. We had to gather up her mother's chickens. I have a hard heart where fowl are concerned. Infuriatingly dumb they are, squawking hysterically when you're trying to save their lives. I've been in an earthquake, too, in California. I was around six, I think. I'd just cracked an egg open when the first tremor struck. For some peculiar reason, I hadn't yet understood how eggs got out of their shells. As it dripped into the sink, there was a great shudder in the little house where my parents had left me to be cared for by an elderly woman. Anyhow, I found myself on the floor. I recall creeping outdoors. A huge cloud of dust was rising in the street. When it cleared, I saw the street had opened up as though it'd been struck by a giant tomahawk."

Elizabeth had made herself a peanut-butter-cracker sandwich while Gran talked. Suddenly, she fell silent. Elizabeth glanced at her. Gran was looking back, an expression of uncertainty on her face. She held the paintbrush in the air as though not only her words had been arrested, but her cleaning.

"I seem to be trying to tell you everything that's ever happened to me," she said, her voice touched with surprise. "You'll end up knowing nearly as much about me as Will did." She gestured toward one of the drawings of Elizabeth's grandfather.

Was she asking for reassurance? Elizabeth didn't want to be the person to give it to her.

Then Gran turned away and went on with her work.

There were difficult moments with Gran— when she had recited that poem about the western wind, and now when she seemed almost apologetic. Elizabeth ate her sandwich. It was hardly fair that along with being shipped away from home, she was expected to make a grown-up feel it was all right to talk about herself. The crackers were stale and the peanut butter dry. Her gloom was coming back, gray like the morning light. But she couldn't sit there silently forever. She cleared her throat.

"Didn't you live with your parents?"

"Barely," Gran said. She came to the table and sat down across from Elizabeth. "My father was an actor. My mother didn't know what a child was. I was left with various people. The old woman in California was one of the nicest."

"Was she mad because you cracked the egg?"

Gran smiled. "She never knew. The earth-quake covered up for me."

"Daddy never told me about your father and mother."

"Family history can get stale—like those crackers—and sink out of sight. And it's not always a bad thing. When you asked me about the storms on the island, I remembered all those natural catastrophes, like a string of fire-crackers going off. I didn't mention the storm at sea." She smiled broadly. Was she making fun of herself? Or of Elizabeth?

"Was your father in the movies?" Elizabeth was interested in that possibility. She imagined her-self telling Nancy that her great-grandfather had been a movie star in the old Gary Cooper days.

"For a few years. He never got more than bit parts. Once he was the second male lead in a play that ran in New York for three months. Not a bad run in those days. He didn't do well at all as an actor. After he and my mother were divorced, he got steady work as manager in a men's clothing store in Boston. The owner thought he'd please the customers. He was so handsome and winsome."

"Did Daddy know them?"

"He met them each several times . . . not the same as knowing them. They both died young, in their fifties." She was looking at Elizabeth intently. "Like Will," she added quietly.

Some emotion of Gran's was about to wash over her and leave her as bare as the wave-scoured boulders on that other, wilder shore. Suddenly, like something glimpsed from the corner of an eye, a picture formed in her mind of a small boy and a young woman, walking slowly down a street, empty save for those two figures. She knew who it was she had imagined in that instant—Gran and Daddy years ago, alone as they had been.

Gran would answer anything she asked. But she wasn't going to ask. She got up and strode across the room to look at the painting on the easel. She wasn't going to feel someone else's feeling. It was too unfair!

Gran came and stood behind her. "That's a watercolor wash," she said. "Ocean, sky, shore. It's mostly what I've been doing lately. Though I am going to make some drawings of you from the snaps I'm taking."

"Will you have a show this year in Camden?" Elizabeth asked, hearing a tremor in her own voice. It came from relief, she knew, that they were talking about something else, not those long-ago days.

"I don't know," Gran said.

Voices, a child laughing, made them both turn to the door. Grace got up from the red sweater and ran across the room to stand near them.

"The Herkimers are taking their daily dip," Gran said.

Through the open door, Elizabeth saw Mrs. Herkimer near the dock, wearing a black bathing suit with a wavy skirt and a long string of pearls. Mr. Herkimer was standing in water up to his knees. The girl who had waggled her fingers at Elizabeth was swimming toward shore. Aaron splashed and laughed in the shallows.

"The boy is the only one having fun," remarked Elizabeth.

"That often appears to be the case," said Gran. "Don't you want to take a swim?"

"I couldn't even wade in that water."

Mr. Herkimer bent and threw water on his face. He looked up blankly. He had a large, fleshy face with a mustache on the upper lip that was so thin he might have drawn it with a pen dipped in black ink. As he plodded awkwardly out of the water, his wife plucked a towel from a canvas bag, shook it, and walked down to him, holding it out. He took it and buried his face in it. Elizabeth decided she didn't like him.

"Can't he get his own towel?" she asked.

"Is it a bad thing that between being born and dying, a person should be handed a towel?" Gran asked coolly.

"I just meant——" Elizabeth began to protest.

But Gran took hold of her arm, interrupting whatever she was going to say. "Let's go out and meet them."

After the introductions were over, Mrs. Herkimer remarked, "You have noticed my pearls, Elizabeth. They're real. I would never, of course, wear anything that wasn't real."

"I can see you're Cora Ruth's grandchild," Mr. Herkimer said to her, but looking at his wife as though to find out if she agreed with him. Deirdre had emerged from the water and was staring up at the ridge, shivering.

"Manners, Deirdre," said her mother. "And put on your robe at once."

"Hello," Deirdre said without looking at Elizabeth.

But Aaron ran out of the water, grinning. "Take my ice-cold hand," he demanded, thrusting it toward her. She barely touched it with her fingertips. "She thinks I'm repulsive," Aaron said gleefully.

"Hush!" commanded Mrs. Herkimer. "Deirdre! What did I tell you? Cover up! You'll get pneumonia. John, will you kindly see to these children?" She turned to Elizabeth. "It's rather nice to see a new face on this splendid shore."

"Can I bring anything for supper?" Gran asked stolidly.

"Don't tell me your ice is holding up!" exclaimed Mrs. Herkimer. "I'm glad that fool is coming tomorrow in his broken-down boat."

"That's a beautiful old launch, Helen," Gran said. "And why on earth do you call Jake a fool?"

"I have my reasons," Mrs. Herkimer said mysteriously.

Deirdre let out a snort of laughter. Aaron began to run in ever-widening circles, shouting, "Grown-ups! Grown-ups!"

"You'll have to take your chances, tonight," Mrs. Herkimer said to Gran and Elizabeth. "I'll throw something together, though you can be sure I'll go to some trouble."

They walked away at last, Mr. Herkimer keeping a firm grip on Aaron's arm as he wriggled like a fish on a hook.

"Does she really want us to come?" Elizabeth asked Gran when the Herkimers were out of earshot.

"Helen usually sounds a bit put out. Pay no mind."

Elizabeth wished she could pay no mind to the kind of things Gran said. What was wrong with Mr. Herkimer having to get his own towel? Oh, it was all too much here! Thinking about what this meant and that meant. Back home, she hardly had to notice her parents. They were just there.

When they went back into the cottage, Gran took an apple from a basket. "I'm going to lie down now. Maybe you'd like to explore this part of the island. Or read." She took a bite of the apple. "I have some books of poetry and some of history, a few on Maine. If you're interested . . ."

"I have books to read for school," Elizabeth said curtly.

Gran went on as though Elizabeth hadn't spoken. "If you go past the Herkimers', you'll find a tiny cemetery. When I had the walls taken down here, I found old newspapers stuck to the laths that must have been used for insulation. The date on one was 1847. That means there have been people on Pring for one hundred forty-five years! There are only three gravestones in the cemetery. The names have worn away except for one." Gran leaned against the table. "Here's a poem to say to yourself when you're there:

"In this little urn is laid
Prudence Baldwin, once my maid
From whose happy spark here let
Spring the purple violet.

"Robert Herrick wrote that around 1640. Perfect, isn't it?"

Gran's smile was pure mischief.

Elizabeth bent to stroke Grace. She had tried to shut her ears as Gran recited. She had clenched herself like a fist. Yet despite her effort, the lines of the poem settled into memory. Brainwashed by my own grandmother, she thought to herself.

She heard Gran going up the stairs. A moment later, her voice floated down. "Don't forget to write a note home. We can send it back with Jake, tomorrow."

There were some sheets of paper on the work-table. Elizabeth took one, and a pencil from one of the jars.

She wrote: I'm here. Gran tells lots of stories. The water's too cold to swim in. I'm okay.

She hesitated, then signed only her name.

5

After writing the note home, Elizabeth looked down at her stingy, graceless lines, folded the paper quickly, and slipped it into an envelope Gran had left for her. Her parents would know she was offended—if they didn't already—but these days, it would hardly matter to them.

She felt listless, as she sometimes did on one of the steely cold days in late November when she came home from school after dull hours in the classroom and could find nothing she wanted to eat in the refrigerator.

In the early dark of such an afternoon, as they met in the kitchen, her mother had told her about the baby that was coming. Elizabeth had felt her knees go weak. The headlights of a car sweeping across the windows had made her blink and cover her face with her hand. Her mother had asked, "Elizabeth? Are you all right?"

She knew she ought to begin reading one of the books on the table upstairs. But, instead, she went out of the cottage into the bright afternoon. She was stuck on the island; she might as well get to know it.

Instead of going past the outhouse to reach the Herkimer place and the cemetery beyond it, she followed the shoreline to that sandy point where the birds came to sit at sunset. The beach on the farther side of the point was composed almost entirely of stones bearded with green waterweed. Above it lay the gradual slope of a meadow of tall grass, through which a path had been worn. The rambling old house sat in a dazzle of sunlight, its weather-beaten clapboard burnished. It was as silent as a monument. Had they all disappeared?

Mr. Herkimer suddenly stepped out of the shadow of the barn and looked intently up at a broken window. She had an impulse to tiptoe past. Then, as had happened in the morning, Aaron sped out of the house; a door slammed. In a second, Mrs. Herkimer appeared. The door slammed again.

"Aaron! Come back here!" she cried. Then they saw Elizabeth. Aaron halted. With both hands, Mrs. Herkimer smoothed down her feathery hair.

"Where are you going?" the little boy shouted.

"None of your business," said Mrs. Herkimer. She smiled distantly at Elizabeth. "He has to know everything," she said.

"I want to *know* everything," Aaron said.

"It's okay. I'm going to take a look at the little cemetery Gran told me about," Elizabeth said.

"You have to take me with you," said Aaron.

From beside the barn, Mr. Herkimer called, "Aaron, don't be always telling people what to do."

Aaron's dark eyes were fixed on Elizabeth's face as though to read it.

"I can be of help," he said seriously. "I know the way."

The Herkimers were silent. Elizabeth had the impression everything was up to her. She hesitated, not wanting the company, or the responsibility, of a small boy, especially such an unpredictable one. The Herkimers were watching her closely now. She felt as though they were resting their combined weight on her.

"He can come with me," she said at last, thinking to herself—just this one time.

"You'll have to watch him every moment," Mrs. Herkimer said, her fingers constantly catching and letting go of her pearls. "He likes to scare one. He likes to jump off high rocks just to startle. He doesn't look where he's going."

Elizabeth had not heard a parent speaking in front of her child as though he wasn't even there. She felt a faint indignation for Aaron's sake, and was glad she had said he could come with her.

"I'll let you watch me," Aaron said. "I'm calm today—easy to watch."

"Go ahead, then," Mrs. Herkimer said. "And behave yourself—"

"Or else!" Aaron cried gleefully. "I know all about *or else*. Come on, Elizabeth!" And he bounded around the house, under a wash line, past a woodpile, and into a grove of slender trees whose white trunks glowed like straight chalk lines among the surrounding pines. Twigs crackled as Aaron ran ahead of her.

"Wait up," she demanded.

He paused to look back at her. His face, dappled in sunlight, then shade, glimmered briefly like a face in a dream. He went on.

She emerged from the little wood to see him streaking across another long, narrow field, bound on one side by the bay, on the other by the slope that led to the crest, bare of trees here, and steeper than it was at the other end of the island. It was forbidding, too, with fanglike black rocks rising from the earth in clusters like the remains of prehistoric creatures.

Aaron stopped beneath a tree whose upheld branches formed the shape of a goblet. He was smiling. A few feet away from where he stood, Elizabeth saw three mossy gravestones, all awry, tumbled like blocks. Aaron put his finger to his lips. "We have to whisper," he said softly. "We mustn't wake them."

"They're dead," Elizabeth stated.

"Dead, but not gone," he retorted.

"You mean, ghosts? Are you trying to scare me?"

"Why? What for?" Aaron asked. "If you got really scared and started screaming, I'd go mad! I'd have to part the waters and escape to the mainland!" He skittered around, searching the ground until he found a stick. He held it up.

"Do you know about Moses' parting the waters of the Red Sea?" he asked. "If the wind was right to help me, I might do the same. After all, Aaron was Moses' brother. Then we could walk across the bay to Molytown."

Elizabeth knelt to look at the gravestones. There were very faint indentations on two of them. On the third, she could make out the dates: 1859–1864. She touched the stone with one finger, tracing the numbers.

"Here's someone who was only five," she said pensively.

"Indian massacre," Aaron declared. "And if it wasn't for us coming, they'd still be here in their swift canoes, hunting giant otters and lobsters as big as dogs."

"You don't know if it was an Indian massacre," she said. "It could have been a disease."

"I'm right," he said. "My uncle Fred told me and he knows all about history and Indians. I'd be with him now if he hadn't gotten sick. They leave me with him every summer, you know, because they think I'm safer there. They don't know Uncle Fred takes me to Mount Baxter. We climb a lot worse rocks than the ones here. Well, what they don't know won't hurt them. Except they'll find out someday. My mother will. She always finds out."

"Why would the Indians have bothered with a tiny island like this?" asked Elizabeth.

"Don't argue," Aaron said. "We can just have our own thoughts." He slid to the ground and leaned against the child's gravestone. "Let's sit here. It's cozy, in a way, and the sun makes me sleepy."

Elizabeth, irritated yet amused, sat down beside him. She hadn't paid attention to young children for a long time, especially small boys, who seemed senseless to her with their running about and shouting and knocking things over.

"Your gran is a spy," Aaron said suddenly.

"What a dumb thing to say!"

"Maybe it's dumb. But I'm right. She spies on us and then goes and draws and paints us when we're not there."

"But she's a painter," Elizabeth protested.

"She made fun of us . . . though I liked the way she painted Deirdre all twisted up, wearing that ugly pink dress."

It was pleasant to sit there in the sun, gulls sailing over the bay, bugs ticking in the grass, a breeze stirring the leaves of the tree.

"Now I'm thinking about how hungry I am," Aaron said.

"I'll give you something else to think about, a poem that's right for this place." She recited the lines about Prudence Baldwin and the purple violet, and was rather pleased when she'd finished.

Aaron was quiet for a moment. Then he said, "If you say 'here let' fast, it sounds like a flower, too. Also, toilet."

She looked at him apprehensively. Was he about to explode into the silliness little kids went in for when they heard certain words, like toilet?

But his expression was serious. "You can do anything with words," he said. "Except eat them. Deirdre says to me, 'I'll make you eat those words.' I can't do that. You can't take them back, either. They sit there like big damp frogs. Why did you come to Pring, anyhow?"

"I was sent away by my parents," Elizabeth replied, and she was startled at the harshness of her own voice.

"I wish my parents would send me away," Aaron said drowsily. "I'd take my canoe a thousand miles from here and build a tepee in the forest."

He had slipped sideways so he was leaning against her. She gazed down at him. His eyes were closed. His dark lashes rested against his pale skin. She moved slightly but he didn't open his eyes. He'd fallen asleep, just like a baby does, suddenly.

For a long time, Elizabeth sat there. Aaron grew heavier as her thoughts grew vaguer. She looked at small clouds on the horizon, at the bay, at the distant line of the mainland. Below her lay the bones of people who had been alive over one hundred years ago, who must have sat in the sun as she and Aaron were doing this day. There had been houses on the island, boats on the shore, the rattle of china, wood smoke from a chimney, a child's voice crying out, perhaps the voice of the child who now lay beneath them. Maybe Aaron was right—dead but not gone. After all, she was thinking about them.

"Say another poem," Aaron demanded as he sat up, yawning.

"That's the only one I know by heart. I'll have to memorize another."

"Bring it tonight," he said. "Else I'll die of boredom."

She laughed.

"It's true. You'll see! Unless Deirdre has a tantrum and throws dishes at me. You're going to have chicken for supper. It's one hundred and twenty years old. Mama never throws anything away. She's crazy."

"You ought not to talk like that about your family," Elizabeth said self-righteously.

"Ho, ho!" cried Aaron, springing to his feet. "You ought to hear the way they talk about me! All night long . . . whispers from the bedroom . . ."

He began to dance around the gravestones the way he had last night when Elizabeth had seen the Herkimers through her bedroom window.

Suddenly, he cried in a falsetto voice, "Settle down, Aaron!"

Elizabeth felt a chill of fear. Maybe he would dart up the crest of the ridge and fling himself into the sea. What if he refused to go home? Would she have to carry him all the way back?

"I'll wake the dead," he said in a tone of voice that suggested he was imitating words he had heard. He sighed then and looked vacantly at the bay.

"Let's go home," he said. "It's time I had my milk and cookies. I'm tired of talking."

He was silent on the way to the Herkimer house, and after he'd opened the screen door and gone inside, he didn't glance back at Elizabeth.

Mrs. Herkimer called from a window, "Thank you for looking after him, Elizabeth. I hope he didn't act like a beast."

"He was fine," Elizabeth answered her crisply. Really, they did behave as though he were a freak! She passed Deirdre, who was lying in the sun on a shabby quilt. A straw hat covered her face. She must have overheard Elizabeth and her mother speaking, but she gave no sign or greeting.

When Elizabeth arrived at the cottage, the big room was empty. She guessed Gran was still resting. She took one of the soft little apples from the basket and ate it, standing next to the sink. Grace came to her and touched her ankle with one paw. She bent to pet her. After a moment, the cat went back to the sweater and curled up. Gran came down the stairs.

"Did you write home?"

"Yes. And I found the cemetery. I took Aaron. The Herkimers sort of made me take him."

"Did you mind?"

"Not really. He's funny. You never know what he's going to say."

Gran nodded. "That may be part of what puzzles his parents," she said. "He speaks what's in his head."

"Grace just touched my leg with her paw to make me pet her. Maybe animals do think. They just can't change their minds."

"Some people would say that if you can't change your mind, you can't think," Gran observed. "It would be better for Aaron if the Herkimers could change their minds about him."

"Don't they love him?" Elizabeth asked.

"They love him because he's theirs," Gran said shortly.

Elizabeth recalled Aaron had asked her for another poem. It made her feel cranky to have to ask Gran to write down "Absence," but she did, if grudgingly.

Gran said she'd do it later, before they left to have supper at the Herkimers'. "Would you like a cup of tea?" she asked. "I feel chilly. The wind is rising."

The sun had disappeared behind gray clouds. Gran began to make a fire in the stove.

"Don't you get tired of having to do that every time you need to boil water?"

"I do," Gran answered. "But if I had a real stove, there would also be electricity and a telephone and sofas. Another good thing out here, there's so little to forget. In Camden, I never can find my keys. I'm always afraid I'll leave a gas burner on, or the lights . . . things like that. It's a part of being old I really hate."

Elizabeth hoped she wouldn't say anything more about being old. It made her uncomfortable in somewhat the same way her friend Nancy did when——as she was given to doing

—she sang all the words of a love song, and Elizabeth couldn't make her stop or even look away from her blissful gaze.

Gran put a dish of ginger cookies on the table. "They're damp. Everything gets damp on the island. I wonder how your little brother is doing. He'll be starting to smile. That makes parents crazy with joy even when they know it's indigestion. I recall your daddy's first smile. He must have been about six weeks old. I was carrying him to the sink to give him a bath."

Gran carrying Daddy! It seemed impossible. But the effort to imagine such a thing distracted her from the pictures of Stephen Lindsay that Gran's words had evoked. Then she thought of Deirdre, mad as a snake, stalking around the place while her parents ceaselessly watched over Aaron.

"Things are not what they seem," she stated, and realized that was something her mother often said.

"You can say that again," Gran agreed.

Elizabeth did. Gran laughed.

Later, she put on one of her cotton dresses. She went to Gran's room to ask her if it was the thing to wear to the Herkimers'.

Gran was standing in front of her little mirror. She was trying on different scarves, holding them close to her face and muttering to herself. She suddenly saw Elizabeth reflected in the mirror.

She smiled in an embarrassed way. "You'd think I'd have gotten accustomed to the way I look," she said. "But I don't seem to have."

Gran was vain!

She took a slip of paper from the bureau and handed it to Elizabeth. It was the poem, "Absence." She read it silently, then held it out to Gran.

"No. I won't take him that," she said. "It's too lonely."

Gran touched her hand without speaking.

6

Against the red glow of the setting sun, the mainland and its scattered villages appeared to be moving, a night train in which passengers, growing aware of the dark, flicked on lights, one by one. It was low tide. From the exposed wet earth rose a powerful smell of mingled salt and iodine. The water made intimate sounds as it withdrew, as if consoling itself.

Gran was wearing the olive and rose scarf she had settled on and was carrying a flashlight. Across the meadow, the Herkimer house glimmered like a cluster of fireflies. The barn was a black shape, already moved into night. It was still easy to see the path through the meadow. Gazing toward the spine of the ridge, Elizabeth saw a yellow bar of sunshine like the light at the bottom of a closed door.

Mr. Herkimer was waiting for them outside. "Welcome," he called in his matter-of-fact voice, and held the door open.

They entered a hall where jackets, coats, and caps hung from hooks in the wall. An old teddy bear sat on the newel post of a staircase, its arms straight up, a button eye hanging from a thread and resting on one cheek like a tear.

To the right was a dining room with a long table and chairs. To the left, the living room. Lit candles and kerosene lamps sat on every surface, even on windowsills. A fire burned in the hearth. On the mantel above it were dozens of framed photographs.

The place could not have been more different from Gran's cottage. Chairs, tables, benches, even a chaise longue, jammed the room. It must have taken many trips on *El Sueño* to transport so much stuff, thought Elizabeth. The tables, too, were crowded with objects of brass and china and tarnished silver, stones in bowls, shells in baskets, and on one table, curling around a lamp, what Elizabeth took to be horse tackle.

Mrs. Herkimer rose grandly from a battered armchair. At the hem of her long green skirt, Elizabeth saw a large hole. Mrs. Herkimer, catching her glance, remarked airily, "Moths . . . moths . . ."

As greetings were exchanged, Elizabeth saw Deirdre sitting on the floor near the fire, staring into the flames. Her T-shirt was wrinkled and dirty and her shorts were several sizes too large.

"Deirdre—for heaven's sake! We have guests," her mother reproached her.

"Hello," Deirdre said with a shake of her wild bramble of brown hair. She didn't turn around to look at anyone.

"For Deirdre, there *are* no occasions. When did you last change your clothes?" Mrs. Herkimer asked the girl's back, but went on at once as though not expecting an answer. "Hasn't the weather been glorious, Cora? Aren't we blessed?"

Gran had remarked to Elizabeth that Mrs. Herkimer gushed over weather, praising the good days as if she were somehow responsible for them.

Mr. Herkimer rubbed his hands together like a fly and asked, "A glass of wine, Cora?"

"Just the thing, John," said Gran.

There was a clatter of feet on the staircase, and in a second Aaron burst into the room. "We're having a party!" he cried, running to Elizabeth and grabbing her around the waist.

"Let go of her, Aaron," ordered Mr. Herkimer. "If you tackle guests like that, they won't come again."

"He's really taken to you," Mrs. Herkimer said. "It's unusual. He hardly likes anyone except his uncle Fred."

"I hate Elizabeth!" yelled Aaron. At once he pressed her hand and whispered, "I don't mean it!"

Mrs. Herkimer ignored the outburst and sat down with Gran on a sofa. Aaron released Elizabeth and wandered over to the table where the seashells were and began to sort them.

"How do you like our little island in the sea?" Mrs. Herkimer asked Elizabeth.

"It's very nice," she answered.

"'Nice,'" repeated Mrs. Herkimer. "A tepid response. Cora, don't you find young people's vocabulary shrinking? Sometimes, of course, they say 'great.' All of John's students do, whether the subject is Batman or Julius Caesar."

Elizabeth was surprised to hear Gran reply that she didn't mind what young people said as long as they read a book now and then. She guessed Gran wouldn't ever show Mrs. Her-

kimer she agreed with her. It would be like
agreeing with Mrs. Herkimer's self-satisfaction.

At that moment, Mr. Herkimer returned
with a tray of glasses of wine, and Mrs. Herkimer excused herself to go to the kitchen.

It was the way evenings were at home when
Elizabeth's mother and father had people to
dinner. They were like sentries guarding their
guests. As soon as one left the room, the other
would appear. When Elizabeth, as occasionally
happened, was invited to stay awhile with the
company, she had discovered that her interest
ebbed away in a few minutes. A thick curtain
seemed to drop between her and the grown-
ups. She heard their voices, but thought about
other things. It was no different tonight. She
stopped listening to Gran and Mr. Herkimer
and went to the fireplace to look at the photographs on the mantel. All of them were
magazine pictures of people skiing or sailing or
riding horses. Deirdre snickered from the floor.

"Those aren't pictures of us," she said. "Mama bought them because she liked the frames."

Elizabeth squatted down so she was close to Deirdre. They stared coolly at each other. "Why are you so mad at me?" Elizabeth asked.

"I don't know you," Deirdre replied. "So I can't be mad at you."

"Elizabeth!" Aaron called.

"Go play with the nut," said Deirdre. For a second, she appeared about to smile. Her mouth twitched. Then she scowled. "You'll be doing me a favor," she said.

Aaron had replaced the shells in the basket. "I have a present for you," he said. He reached into a pocket and took out a metal giraffe, its brown spots nearly faded away. "He can see over the trees, over this island, to everywhere," he said. He pressed the giraffe against her palm. "Hide it!" he commanded her. She slipped it into the pocket of her dress.

"Dinner is ready," announced Mrs. Herkimer from the hall.

Elizabeth had never seen so much cutlery and so many plates piled on a table. At each place was a paper napkin printed with clowns, probably left over from a birthday. A small pale chicken lay carved upon an oval platter, and two silver dishes held watery beets and string beans. There was a basket of sliced white bread and a large bowl of steaming potatoes.

Aaron insisted that Elizabeth sit next to him, and when she sat, he began to bang the table with a fork and jiggle around in his chair. Mr. Herkimer told him to calm down and placed a potato on his plate.

Aaron looked down at it. He said in a loud, solemn voice, "This is what I've wanted all my life."

Elizabeth burst into laughter.

"Good!" cried Aaron, and clapped his hands.

"Aaron is very theatrical," said Mrs. Herkimer as she sat down.

"He's an attention hog," said Deirdre.

"Oink! Oink!" squealed Aaron.

Except for the potatoes, the food was dreadful. Gran ate small bites of chicken very slowly. She caught Elizabeth's glance and rolled her eyes upward.

"This is a plain American meal," declared Mrs. Herkimer, as though there might be doubt about what it was. "Honest food is all I have time for. Reading and reports for the historical society take up all my strength. Then, of course, I have my family. Before we return to Orono, I have to complete a report on nineteenth-century prison life in Maine."

"A good subject for you," Gran murmured.

"Oh, Cora! Do you remember when you first came to Pring?" Mrs. Herkimer cried. "I was painting then, too, but I hardly have the leisure now for such hobbies."

In a voice as hard as crystal, Gran said, "Painting is not a hobby."

Mr. Herkimer cleared his throat loudly. "Have you noticed those plastic bottles washing up on our shores this summer, Cora?" he asked. "Twice as many as last year. They'll never sink. . . ."

Aaron was pulling on Elizabeth's arm.

"I only eat potatoes, cookies, canned pears, and tea, and one glass of milk a day," he said. "When you have me to supper, that's what you have to give me."

"I'll never have you to supper," Elizabeth replied, smiling.

"Lucky you," Deirdre said.

"Listen to what Deirdre likes to eat," Aaron said. "Worms! Green ones from the sand, and oozy red ones from the ground. Ugh!"

"I'll make you eat those words!" Deirdre threatened.

"See!" he said triumphantly to Elizabeth. "I told you she'd say that!"

"Children. In the words of the poet—shut up!" said Mr. Herkimer mildly.

"Do you enjoy sailing?" Mrs. Herkimer asked Elizabeth. Before she could answer, Mrs. Herkimer continued, "My people were, so to speak, born to the mast. My grandfather used to sail out of Newport—"

"He used to sail out of the local bar three sheets to the wind," muttered Deirdre.

"And win any race he entered," Mrs. Herkimer went on blandly, ignoring Deirdre's words. "But I must say, John has become quite a good sailor even though he was born in western Ohio and never saw the sea until I showed it to him."

"You can last in these waters exactly one hundred twenty seconds," Mr. Herkimer said cheerfully to Elizabeth, as if he were telling her good news. "It's been timed, though I can't think how. The fog is the other menace. It will seem perfectly clear. First there's a haze, and suddenly you're enveloped. Can't see your hand in front of your face."

"Maine sailing was my own father's specialty," Mrs. Herkimer said. "Cora, didn't you have a little sailing dinghy once?"

"Helen, you've forgotten. I sold it years ago in Molytown. My arthritis got so bad."

"And then you're so busy with your little paintings," Mrs. Herkimer said in a fruity voice.

For a moment, Gran looked grim. Then she smiled, as though someone had whispered a joke into her ear. "That's right, Helen," she said. "No time for hobbies like sailing."

"Perhaps Elizabeth will come with us on our boat one of these days," suggested Mr. Herkimer.

"You'll have to wear a life jacket," Aaron whispered to her. "But it won't matter if the ship goes down. We'll all freeze to death, anyhow."

"And what grade are you in?" Mrs. Herkimer asked Elizabeth, a question asked her by grown-ups as far back as she could recall, and which always seemed more significant to them than her name.

"I go into the sixth in September," she answered.

"Only the sixth?" Mrs. Herkimer said thoughtfully. "I would have imagined—Deirdre is already in the tenth. Of course, she skipped a grade. It may be a problem for her to graduate at sixteen. . . . "

"You're boasting, Helen," Mr. Herkimer admonished her in a tentative way, as though he were only half-serious.

"Boast? Me?" exclaimed Mrs. Herkimer. "Why, I'm the least boastful person in the entire world!"

Mr. Herkimer passed around food, but no one, not even Mrs. Herkimer, took second helpings. Deirdre was pushing a string bean from one side of her plate to the other. Mrs. Herkimer began to complain about Jake Holborn, how he rammed their dock more often than he used to, and was damaging it. "He's too old to run that boat," she said. "I think he should retire. He's certainly stuffed a mattress full of money by now, after all these years."

"I don't think so," Gran said firmly. "He only delivers to one or two other islands besides Pring."

"Mama! He's poor!" Deirdre said indignantly. "I remember that time we stopped by his trailer to order some lobsters when we were on our way here. His place looked like an old freight car."

"Our little socialist," Mrs. Herkimer said.

"I'd like to live on a train," Aaron told Elizabeth. "I'd be the passenger who never gets off."

"You'd get bored," said Elizabeth.

"No," he disagreed. "I'd have the whole car to myself. I'd only invite certain people to visit and have tea. If you got on my train, I'd ask you to stay."

"If the conductors found out you were on one of their trains, they'd make sure the car was pushed onto a siding. Then it would rust, and weeds would grow as high as the windows, and stray cats would be your only visitors," said Deirdre.

"Perfect!" said Aaron delightedly.

Gran had begun to tell a story about being locked out of a house. The children fell silent to listen.

"My father got a part in a gangster movie— just a small part, really—but on the strength of it, he and my mother rented a house in Hollywood. I recall it had a waterfall you could turn on and off with a switch. I was living then with my aunt Emma. They sent for me, and Aunt Emma and I went west on the train. While she was in San Diego visiting a friend, I renewed my acquaintance with my parents. They went out the first night I was there, leaving me alone. I must have gotten worried, or curious, and I went out the front door of that big house. The door slammed shut and locked itself. So there I was, about six, I think, in the Hollywood Hills."

Aaron gasped. "I'd like to get locked out," he whispered excitedly to Elizabeth.

"Anytime," Deirdre said.

"I ran into the garden to look at that waterfall," Gran was saying. "My father had neglected to switch it off before they left for their party. The water fell into a big pool full of goldfish. Something about the dark garden, the falling water, the orange glimmer of fish, must have startled me. I ran back to the front of the house. I had begun to be scared. Soon, a man came along who'd heard the waterfall and thought he'd left his lawn sprinkler on. He took me to his house, and his wife cut up a banana and poured cream on it to give to me. She put me to bed. I can still see the quilt she covered me with, its diamonds of bright colors, though it's sixty-eight years since I last saw it."

"Heavens, Cora!" exclaimed Mrs. Herkimer. "My parents would never have left me alone!"

"There's another part to the story," Gran went on. "Before Elizabeth was born, when my son and her mother were living with me in the farm-house, I locked myself out for the second time in my life. I'd gone to a painter friend's opening and party in Boston. I got home around two A.M. It was winter and very cold, and I'd misplaced my house key. Elizabeth's father, my dear son, let me in. Now and then, life balances out."

"Could you tell that story again?" asked Aaron.

"When you come to visit me," Gran said.

Mrs. Herkimer rose. "I've made blueberry duff from an old family recipe," she said.

"Help your mother clear, Deirdre," ordered Mr. Herkimer.

"Do I have to?"

"No. You can retire to your room instead."

Elizabeth was preoccupied. Why did she feel so uneasy? Was it because Gran had looked only at her as she talked? Was it because Gran had revealed how different her life was from other people's lives?

She shouldn't have told the Herkimers—especially the Herkimers—about being left alone and locked out. Wasn't being a painter different enough? Yet everyone had paid attention to her. And Mrs. Herkimer had even appeared to be interested.

She had walked back into the dining room by then, carrying a dish crowded with squares of dough covered with blueberries. "My specialty," she said as she set down the dish.

"But what did your daddy say when he couldn't find you after he got home?" Aaron asked.

"That's still another part of the story," Gran said, smiling at him. "I'll tell you another time."

"I was so fortunate in my parents," Mrs. Herkimer said with a long, gratified sigh.

"Yes," Deirdre snapped. "You might have been born in an old trailer and had some lady swear your mattress was full of money when you couldn't afford to buy one of your own lobsters!"

"Deirdre, that will do!" said Mr. Herkimer sternly.

"I think the sky is so starry tonight we might not need our flashlight," Gran said quickly.

His mouth full of dessert, Aaron said to Elizabeth, "Let's go back to the cemetery tomorrow."

"We'll see," she replied.

"You sound like one of *them*," he complained.

She started to protest, but Gran, Deirdre, and the Herkimers were moving into the entrance hall. Aaron stayed in his chair, picking blueberries out of the dough squares and stuffing his mouth with them. Elizabeth joined the others. Mrs. Herkimer drew her aside at once.

"Aaron really does like you," she said. "If you could keep him company once in a while, you could think of it as a summer job—we'd pay you—"

"You won't pay her," Gran said, walking to where they were standing.

Elizabeth felt a flash of resentment. It wasn't up to Gran. At the same time, she knew she was right. And in any case, she didn't want to be a baby-sitter on Pring Island.

Deirdre was gesturing at her. She went to the staircase, where the girl was leaning against the newel post, holding the teddy bear in one hand. She didn't seem to be aware of how fiercely she was clutching it.

"You really are lucky," she said in a low voice. Her face worked as though she were thinking very hard. Then she said, as Elizabeth stood there awkwardly, "Your luck is that you weren't born into a family that thinks it's more wonderful than any other family in the history of the world."

Elizabeth still felt the surprise of Deirdre's words as she and Gran walked through the meadow. When they were well out of earshot of the Herkimer house, she said, "That's some bunch of people! They all seem crazy except Mr. Herkimer, and he's like their keeper."

Gran laughed and the sound of her laughter was comforting in the cool dark night. She had turned on the flashlight after all. The vast sky glimmered through a thin cloud cover. "Families are pretty crazy when you see them close up," she said.

They had reached the stony beach. Water lapped softly.

"Is Deirdre always so angry?"

"When I first knew her, she was like a sweet bird playing in the meadow. A merry little girl. Growing up is hard, and then there's their absorption in Aaron."

"I'll never be like Deirdre," Elizabeth said.

"Don't say 'never,' Elizabeth," Gran said.

They rounded the sand spit. The cottage rose before them, a small, black cliff. Grace meowed nearby.

"Oh!" Gran exclaimed. "I locked her out!"

"When you came home that morning in Hollywood, what did your parents say?"

"As I recall," Gran said, "they didn't notice I'd been gone."

⚛7⚛

El *Sueño* arrived at the Herkimer dock, which was larger and sturdier than Gran's, early the next morning.

Everyone gathered in silence, after muttered "good mornings," to observe the boat's slow approach into the cove. Elizabeth thought, We're just like the birds that come to sit on the sand spit in the late afternoons.

They all came closer to the dock as a thin boy of fifteen or so moved quickly to tie up the boat and began to unload boxes and bags of groceries and bundles of mail. Old Jake Holborn would point wordlessly to a box. The boy would heft it and dump it from deck to dock.

Jake looked much older than Gran. A black watch cap covered his head. His dark blue sweatshirt was spotted with paint stains. Elizabeth

noted the much-knotted laundry string that
threaded the eyelets of his old-fashioned sneakers. An unlit cigarette hung from the corner of
his mouth.

"I don't see my eggplant," complained Mrs.
Herkimer.

"I couldn't find none," Jake said, the cigarette bobbing as he spoke. "Eggplant shortage
all over the state of Maine." Mrs. Herkimer
looked offended.

Aaron darted to Elizabeth's side. "Come and
get me as soon as you can," he said. "We'll go
to the cemetery."

"When I'm able to," she said with a touch of
irritation. He would gobble up all her time if
she let him. He was watching her face closely.

"Please," he asked mournfully.

"Okay. In a while," she said.

The Herkimers were trailing across the
meadow with their supplies. Jake Holborn came

over to Gran. "This is your grandchild?" he asked, staring at Elizabeth.

"Indeed she is," Gran replied.

"Looks like you in a way," he said. "Greeley, help these folks take their stuff to the cottage."

"Would you like a cup of tea, Jake?" Gran asked.

"No time today, Cora. I've got two more islands. Some new people over at Staghead with what looks to be about twenty kids."

"I've nearly finished the drawing of *El Sueño*," Gran told him. "I'll have it for you next trip."

The old man's face lit up with his smile, and the cigarette fell out of his mouth. He caught it with his spotty, gnarled hand. "That'll be nice," he said. "A comfort when winter comes."

Later, after he and the silent Greeley had chugged out of the cove, and Gran was putting away groceries, Elizabeth asked to see the drawing. Gran went to look among her canvasses and sketchbooks. She found what she was searching for and handed it to Elizabeth.

Taped to a pasteboard was a drawing of *El Sueño*, Jake in his watch cap standing on the deck.

"Someone in Molytown actually owns the launch," Gran explained. "But Jake can't help but feel it's his. He's been running the service to the islands for thirty years. I know he's scared about how much longer he can manage. He asked me to take a few snapshots of the launch. I decided to do a drawing, too."

"Does he have children?"

"None. He's alone."

"Aaron asked me to go with him to the cemetery again."

"Do you want to? You're not obliged, you know."

"I like him all right, but not feeling I have to spend time with him."

"It's up to you, Elizabeth. Maybe you can be a substitute sister. One of these days, Deirdre might stop being horrible. I'm going to work now. You can have a big lunch today. Fresh eggs, tomatoes, Swiss cheese, among other good things."

Gran went across the room into her work territory. It was as if she had left the cottage.

Elizabeth went to her room and opened *To Kill a Mockingbird*. But she couldn't concentrate. Her glance strayed to the windows. She caught sight of the sparkle of water, the dark vigorous green of pine boughs. She didn't see how she was going to get through two novels before school began. She used to read all the time. This last year, something had changed. Every book was a heavy weight. She was struck by an idea. She could read one of them to Aaron.

After looking at the first chapters, she decided the Hemingway story might hold Aaron's attention. Short sentences for short boys, she told herself.

After she'd made a sandwich and eaten it, she left the cottage. Gran didn't look up as Elizabeth went out the door.

The island looked washed clean, as if the tide had risen to cover it briefly, then left it to dry in the sun. At the Herkimer house, Aaron was waiting for her, sitting on the ground, a sack of cookies balanced on one knee.

"You came! I've been waiting a hundred hours!" he cried.

Mrs. Herkimer came to the screen door.

"We don't want to impose on you, Elizabeth," she said. "My family never imposes. Are you sure you want to play with Aaron?"

"And be responsible for him," Mr. Herkimer said as he joined his wife. "Is that too heavy a responsibility perhaps, even for a serious girl like you?"

"I'm light as a feather," Aaron said.

"I want to," Elizabeth said in what was nearly a shout. At the moment, she found the Herkimers unbearable and wished only to get away from them.

"For God's sake! What can happen to him on this stupid pile of rocks and gull guano?" Deirdre's exasperated voice came from somewhere above. Elizabeth looked up and saw her sitting in the crotch of a small oak, a book in one hand.

"Don't speak so coarsely, Deirdre," said Mrs. Herkimer. "Elizabeth will think we're a low family."

Aaron suddenly leaped up and took off to the back of the house, and Elizabeth followed, hearing the Herkimers calling Aaron's name reproachfully. There was a mocking falsetto echo of their voices from Deirdre.

"Here's a game," Aaron said as she caught up with him beneath one of the white-barked trees. He stood with his arms circling the thin trunk. "In the cemetery, you can pretend to be an Egyptian mummy. I'll dig you up—then you'll tell me what it was like in those olden days."

He let go of the tree and raced on ahead of her.

"I don't know about mummies and Egypt," Elizabeth cried after him. He paused and turned.

"Make it up," he ordered. "You just need a little bit of a thing to start a story. Pretty soon, there's everything!"

He jumped over a fallen branch and ran on. As she emerged from the woods, he streaked across the long meadow. When Elizabeth reached the little cemetery, he was reclining against a gravestone, chewing a stem of grass.

"Ready?" he asked.

Elizabeth lay flat on the ground and crossed her arms over her chest. She shut her eyes against the blue glare of the cloudless sky.

"I'm sure there's a mummy here," Aaron said loudly. "You assistants be careful as you dig! More to the left! There it is!"

Suddenly, his breath was warm against her ear as he whispered, "Now you have to sit up. Begin to talk."

Elizabeth slowly raised herself from the waist.

"Look, men! The mummy is alive," he cried.

Elizabeth stifled a laugh that was rising in her throat like a bubble in a bottle. She felt nervous, too, as though she had to speak a part in a play she hadn't learned.

"I am an old Egyptian," she began in a deep voice. "I live by the Nile River. In the mornings, the crocodiles come up to sun themselves on the banks."

"What did you have for breakfast?" Aaron asked as he sat down on the ground in front of her.

"Cornflakes, burned toast, and blueberry jam."

"Oh, Elizabeth!"

"All right . . . all right. I had coconuts and dates."

"Good! And after, did you play with all your friends, the other mummies?"

"I played with all my friends," Elizabeth intoned.

"What?" he asked impatiently. "What did you play?"

"Chariots," she said. "We have toy chariots and we race them and the crocodiles watch. Then we do our schoolwork on papyrus sheets. Then we have lunch."

"What's papyrus?"

"It's a kind of paper made from water plants."

He had been watching her intently, but now his gaze grew unfocused. She could see interest fading from his face like light dimming in a room. He looked down at the bay.

"Could you take me out in our sailboat?" he asked. "I know what to do if a storm comes up.

Daddy said you have to tie yourself to the mast and let the sail fly. That way you won't be washed out to sea."

"I don't know how to sail," she said.

"We could find a bigger island. We could get lost and build a shelter of branches."

"I really can't sail," she said.

After that, they went toward the ridge. Elizabeth found still another path, this one with a few rough-hewn stone steps at the steepest part. Had those early settlers built them to be able to reach the sea more easily?

It was thrilling to go from the peaceful meadow, over the ridge, to the black rocks, to hear the boom of the water as it rolled across the stones, into coves, snaking into deep crevices and sending spray high into the air.

They drifted along the shore, sometimes together, mostly apart. For a long time, they sat at the edge of a tidal pool sunk into the middle of a large boulder. Through greenish scum, they saw tiny crabs move with mysterious haste, and tiny fish like grains of rice dart in and out of clumps of weed. The sun was like a hot towel pressed to their heads and shoulders. Abruptly, Aaron said he had to go home, he was hungry. They must have been together for hours by then.

A picture of the kitchen in her own home flashed in Elizabeth's mind, and she felt restless, suddenly bored. She was glad to leave that harsh, glittering place.

When they came to the stone steps, Aaron asked, "Do you think stones can feel us walking on them?"

She replied that she didn't know.

In the cottage later, she repeated his question to Gran. "Stones are inorganic, without life," Gran said. "At least, as far as is known."

"Aaron sees the smallest things. I get tired of so much noticing."

"It's a way of making a private world," Gran said, and drank from her mug of tea.

"You said he liked the poem about Prudence Baldwin," she said a moment later. "I've written down another by Robert Frost that's even shorter. Maybe I'll find a one-liner before you go home. Here." She reached into a pocket and took out a scrap of paper that she handed to Elizabeth. The two lines were printed in pencil:

We dance round in a ring and suppose,
But the Secret sits in the middle and knows.

Elizabeth read it.

"Aaron's a secret," she said.

"Aren't we all?" Gran asked in a weary voice. Elizabeth stared at her. Her head drooped. Her skin was pale. Gran looked back at her. "I'll go lie down," she said almost shyly. "I worked too long, I think."

Elizabeth watched her as she climbed the stairs, one hand gripping the rope banister, the other pressed against the wall.

For a few minutes, Elizabeth sat motionless at the table, hearing again Gran's words: "a one-liner before you go home." She had been angry at home, and angry here on Pring.

She had wanted to bicycle away with Nancy to escape the grip of anger that woke with her in the mornings, and kept her awake at night when Stephen Lindsay's cries sent her parents whirling through the house.

Though it was only the third day she had been on the island, the grip had loosened. As she gazed around the room that had, at first glance, looked so strange, even senseless, it seemed almost beautiful, almost like a person she had begun to love.

SOME MORNINGS, Elizabeth woke up before Gran. She had learned to start a fire in the stove.

She heated water and let out Grace. She would stand in the doorway gazing at the rippling bay until the cat came back, meowing for her breakfast.

In the late afternoons, she watched the shadows of the columns lengthening on the floor until dusk had flowed into every corner of the room, and Gran began to light the lamps.

After breakfast, Gran sketched her, mostly referring to the Polaroid snaps she'd taken, but occasionally glancing at Elizabeth from her worktable, as though she were a tree. Elizabeth had lost her self-consciousness. She went about whatever she was doing, hardly aware of Gran's hand moving over her sketch pad.

Gran often told stories about her own childhood, her elusive parents, the variety of jobs she'd had as a young woman who had to support herself, and about living in France for a year. She talked about discovering her desire to become an artist, and her early years with Elizabeth's grandfather.

Now, when Elizabeth looked at Gran's sketches of Will Benedict, she had the uncanny sensation that he was looking back at her, that —as she learned more and more about him— he was learning more about her. From under the brim of his rakish hat, he seemed to stare at her interestedly.

On some mornings, Gran was brisk, strong, and laughed often. There were other days when she was silent, grim, and moved with increasing difficulty as the hours advanced, until all at once, she would sink in a chair and stare down at her hands.

On one such morning, the few words she spoke seemed meant only for herself. "There are tribes that don't let themselves be photographed," she said. "They believe the camera can steal their souls. I've come to think your soul should be stolen, all of it used up by the time you leave the world."

There were moments when Elizabeth wished Gran was only talking to herself. She would pounce on some casual thing Elizabeth said, for instance, when she described her math teacher as "really neat."

"Do you mean *tidy?*" Gran asked irritably. "What on earth *do* you mean? Children say 'really neat' about everything—hamburgers, music, horror films. . . ."

On a morning when Elizabeth padded downstairs with the laces of her sneakers untied, Gran stared at them with a grimace. "For goodness' sake, tie up your shoes," she said. "You look like you're unraveling."

"Everybody in school wears them this way."

"Everybody!" exclaimed Gran. "Don't you want to be an individual? I saw a rock singer on television wearing a baseball cap backward. Next day when I went to the grocer's, all the people I saw under twenty were wearing their caps backward. We've become a nation of sheep."

"Maybe you shouldn't watch TV," Elizabeth said angrily.

Gran's face softened. "I'm sorry," she said. "You're right. The world is so different now. But I do believe that when language shrinks, brains do, too."

Elizabeth wondered, at those uncomfortable moments, what her father's life as a child had been like. Had Gran spoken to him in that impatient way?

She spent a part of every day with Aaron. They met in the cemetery. For a while, he was agreeable to being read to, although he interrupted her with questions: Why is the old man so sad? What's a marlin? Why do the other fishermen laugh at the old man? Until finally, she cried out in exasperation, "Aaron! You talk more than you listen."

"I must know everything," he answered. "Anyhow," he said as he jumped up and began his dance around the gravestones, "I'm tired of that story."

It was the end of reading *The Old Man and the Sea* aloud. But by then, Elizabeth had become interested and went on to finish the book by herself.

She recited the poem Gran had written down. Aaron seemed elated by it. "'The Secret sits in the middle and knows,'" he repeated, shouting the words louder and louder until they seemed to fill the meadow and roll up to the foot of the ridge.

One afternoon, Elizabeth passed Deirdre sitting on the Herkimer dock.

"How come you're not with my adorable little brother?" she called out.

Elizabeth halted. "He is adorable," she said. "But you aren't especially."

Deirdre stood and looked at Elizabeth somberly. "You don't know anything about me," she said. "The truth is, I'm *glad* you're here. I'm *glad* he follows you around like a dog!"

She walked past Elizabeth and through the meadow without a backward look.

On a rainy day, Aaron came to the cottage carrying a stained canvas bag full of cookie crumbs and a set of dominoes. Whenever he matched a domino of his with one of Elizabeth's, he exploded into laughter, jumped up from the floor near the fireplace where they were sitting, and ran around the room. "Honestly, Aaron, cool off, will you? This is no fun," Elizabeth protested.

Gran quickly painted a mask for him with watercolors. It was half lamb, half wolf. Elizabeth made two holes in it and passed a string through them. He stood humbly before her, his shoulders bent, as she tied it around his head. But at once, he began to growl and bleat. He refused to take the mask off until Elizabeth had made tea and filled a basket with cookies. Gran had gone upstairs for her nap.

"I like your house better than mine," Aaron said, his mouth full. "Can I see your room?"

She took him upstairs. He peered into her room as though it were an exhibit in a museum with a velvet cord in front of the door.

"That's your little bed," he said. "You can look out at the moon from those little windows. And there's the book you read to me."

"The book you wouldn't let me read to you."

He grinned, and they went back downstairs.

"Your gran is an old hippie," he said suddenly.

Elizabeth, startled, laughed. "What's that supposed to mean?" she asked. He must have heard someone say it.

"I don't know," he replied vaguely. He wandered to Gran's workplace. "Look at the launch!"

he exclaimed. "And Jake's there on the deck! I can't draw a circle. How does a person draw anything?"

When Aaron had gone home, and Gran came downstairs to start supper, Elizabeth told her what he had said. Gran smiled broadly.

"It was your father who was the hippie," she said.

"Daddy!" exclaimed Elizabeth.

"Oh, yes. For a year or two, his hair was down past his shoulders. The farmhouse used to thump with rock music."

"I can't believe it," said Elizabeth. She didn't know a great deal about hippies except what she'd picked up from movies. Lots of men had long hair now, lanky ponytails snaking down the jackets of their business suits.

"He wasn't a serious hippie," Gran said. "At least, not for long. Then he started law school . . . you came along. His mind just turned to other things."

"Daddy, with long hair," Elizabeth said wonderingly. "Wait till I tell him I know!"

Gran smiled. "He'll get after me," she said.

"But why did Aaron say you were a hippie?"

"Helen must have said it, though she'd never admit that. She likes to think she's a woman of the world. I know that, secretly, she suspects artists are dangerous."

"Why?"

Gran sighed deeply. Her mood seemed to change. "Because they are, I suppose," she said almost curtly.

She put two bowls of thick soup on the table, muttered, "Bread . . . bread . . ." to herself, and reached to a shelf for a loaf, her fingers fumbling with the slippery plastic wrapper. After a moment, she managed to extract several slices and drop them onto a dish. She sighed again and sat down at the table, glancing at Elizabeth, who was holding Grace. For a moment, she looked blank, then smiled ruefully. "Little things can get you down," she said.

Grace growled. Elizabeth realized she had been gripping her tightly. She put her on the floor and went to the table. They ate their soup in silence.

Who was this old woman who sat across from her? She had been the visitor on holidays, her father's mother, someone who was nearly always at ease, who often irritated her own mother. Someone who once, when Elizabeth's parents were out, had given her a lunch consisting only of ice cream. Elizabeth's thoughts spun like a top. She struggled to make that pale old person, thinking her own thoughts across the table from her, the familiar Gran about whom she need not think.

There was enough on her mind. Mainly Aaron. He had begun to seem fragile to her, someone to be protected. But against what?

Yesterday, when he had ended their time together—as he usually did—by announcing that he was hungry and had to go home at once, she had paused at the screen door of his house to peer after him.

He hadn't raced to the kitchen as she had imagined he would, but had gone straight to his mother, who was standing in the gloom of the hallway, polishing some object with a rag. He had clasped her about the waist, desperately, it had seemed to Elizabeth. Mrs. Herkimer had bent to enfold him in her arms. They had stood that way for long moments.

"Aaron is like one of those butterflies the wind blows about," she said suddenly.

Gran looked up. "Or like someone born without a skin," she said.

"Yes," Elizabeth agreed, and felt a rush of affection for Gran that left her untroubled for a little while.

SHE TAUGHT Aaron to play blindman's buff but discovered that when it was her turn to be blindfolded with the scarf she'd borrowed from Gran, she was afraid to let him out of her sight. She tore the scarf from her head.

After that, he had to be the blindman so she could keep watch on him. He didn't seem to mind.

One afternoon, he ran away from her. She went to all the places where they played, her panic growing. After an hour, she ran to the cottage, wanting to tell Gran she had lost him before she had to tell the Herkimers.

He was there, talking with Gran on the path leading to the dock.

"Aaron!" she cried furiously. "How could you be so bad? You scared me to death!"

He grinned and shrugged. "You sound like Deirdre," he said cheerfully. "I wanted to see if I could hand you the slip."

"Give you the slip," Gran corrected. She, too, appeared cheerful, untouched by Elizabeth's upset.

"I'm not like Deirdre," Elizabeth protested.

"Sometimes you are," he said.

The westering sun made the sky glow. The worshiping birds were sitting in a line on the sand spit, their beaks gleaming.

"How beautiful it is," murmured Gran.

Grace came around the house to them. Suddenly, she flattened herself on the ground. "Why is she doing that?" Aaron asked.

"She feels all that immensity above us," Gran said.

"An eagle could fly down and snatch her away," Aaron said, dropping to the ground beside the cat. Gran took Grace to the cottage. Elizabeth grabbed Aaron and lifted him up so that she was holding him close to her. She could feel his heart beating.

"No eagle will get you," she said. It seemed as if her own heart would overflow with gratitude that he was safe.

"Let me go!" he cried out in a sharp, unhappy voice.

Aghast, she put him down. A stream of words burst from him.

"They're always grabbing me, picking me up, shaking me. They're always asking me where I'm going and where I've been and what I'm doing and what I'm thinking . . . and am I sleepy . . . and did I remember to put socks on . . . and did I wash my hands, and did I change my wet shoes, and when I come home from school, one of them is waiting so close to the road I think they'll get run over by the bus . . . and Deirdre is always barking and yelling and telling me she'll kill me if I go into her room. Her room! Yow! Her horrible room! And why don't I look at this book and that book and every book, and do I feel hot or cold . . ." His voice trailed off. He was staring at Elizabeth as though seeing straight through her.

Gradually, he seemed to find her again. "Sometimes when someone hugs me," he said softly, "I feel like an eagle has got me in its claws."

"Talons," Elizabeth muttered.

"Talons," he repeated gravely.

8

"**I** try to cultivate Spartan virtues," said Mrs. Herkimer, walking into the water until it reached her ankles.

"I don't have a one," Gran called from the shore.

Elizabeth wasn't sure what Spartan virtues were, but she knew they were both boasting.

She no longer attempted to swim. The cold was too intense. But she had come to love the bay, its changing colors and long tides, the birds whose flight strung black lines across the sky, and cormorants that often landed on a giant boulder at one side of the cove to stretch out their wings for the sun to dry.

Herring gulls flocked behind the fishing boats that went out from Molytown every day. Gray and white shorebirds on their wire-thin legs dashed behind retreating waves in search of food like so many pairs of hard-working scissors. She had seen seals swimming close to shore, a gleam of dark eyes in brown dough faces, and in the long, quiet afternoons, heard the busy hammer of a woodpecker in the woods.

On an early evening toward the end of her third week on the island, she ambled over to the Herkimer dock and sat down, her legs dangling just above the water. It was high tide and the gangway to the Herkimer sailboat was level. The air was cool; in the west, the sky held a tinge of red. Back home, an hour without something to do or someone to talk to had seemed to Elizabeth a waste of time, a kind of failure. She had discovered that she liked to be alone and idle. So she felt faintly disappointed when she heard voices drifting across the meadow.

Shortly, Mr. Herkimer appeared, holding Aaron by the hand.

"He saw you and wanted to come out and say good-night," he said.

Aaron was wearing bright red pajamas and a large pair of flopping sneakers that must have belonged to his father. He sat down beside her. Mr. Herkimer went over to the sailboat.

"There's the first star," Elizabeth said. "It's millions of miles away."

"Maybe it's only one hundred feet away," he said.

Elizabeth laughed. "Then we could touch it, nearly."

"No," Aaron said firmly. "Because we might be as small as sand fleas. We might be the fleas of fleas. We don't know how big or small we are."

From the sailboat, Elizabeth heard either a groan or a muffled laugh.

"You'd better make up your mind," Elizabeth said. "We are either big, or we're tiny."

"I never can make up my mind," Aaron said. He was quiet for a moment. Then, in a whisper, he asked, "When you go away, will I ever see you again?"

It was a shock to think of leaving the island. Before Aaron had come to sit beside her, she had felt in her right place, like the island itself. But she had been jarred out of place by his question, reminded of time, reminded that the coolness of the air was not merely the weather of evening but a portent of autumn.

"You can't tell," she said at last. "Maybe I'll come back next summer."

"If my uncle is better, they'll want me to stay with him," Aaron said quietly, without resentment.

"We'll have to see," she said.

He stood up in his abrupt way. "Good-night," he said. "I'll see you tomorrow."

Mr. Herkimer was standing close by. "You go ahead to the house, Aaron," he said. "I'll watch you."

"Don't watch me!" protested Aaron as he ran off the dock, the too-large sneakers thumping on the boards.

Mr. Herkimer remained. Elizabeth stood up, feeling uneasy.

"We . . . I . . . want to thank you," he said. "It's been good for Aaron . . . spending these days with you." He paused a moment. "Deirdre can't help but be angry because of the time we give to Aaron. But we must . . . we must."

Elizabeth was mute. What could she say? She didn't want to be thanked. How she wished Mr. Herkimer would go away!

A second later, he did, calling out a faint, sad "good-night" over his shoulder.

She went back slowly to the cottage. She had grown used to being outside in the dark, used to the outhouse with its loop of rustling ivy leaves.

She liked the evening sponge baths, the wait while water heated on the stove, the lighting of the lamps. She had said to Gran that she had grown to love this way of living. But Gran said when you chose it, it was entirely different from having it forced on you. "Only well-off people can afford to be poor for a lark," she had said, and laughed as though gratified by a joke she had made.

The best things of all were the long, slow talks with Gran as they nibbled on cookies when supper was over, the plates washed and wiped and put away. The smell of Gran's paints seemed to intensify in the evening. A new seascape might be on the easel. Grace would be sleeping on the sweater, or else purring as she wound softly around their ankles like a piece of silk.

Gran's stories of her life, of Elizabeth's father when he was a boy, seemed to spring from an endless source.

"Don't you run out sometimes?" Elizabeth asked.

Gran didn't answer at once. "I like telling you about the past," she said. "It's as if it is happening again."

Often, Elizabeth paused in front of the portraits of Will Benedict. "Maybe I overdid that one a little," Gran had said once when she saw Elizabeth staring at the drawing of her grandfather in his hat. "He was a romantic-looking man. But that one, with the hat, I did from memory. He never looked that desperate. It was me that was desperate, trying to make him come back to life."

It was entirely dark now. Elizabeth opened the cottage door. The big room was empty. She shivered as apprehension took hold of her, a sense that Gran was nowhere in the house.

On the table, she saw a chocolate bar and, underneath it, a note.

I'll miss our evening together, it read. I got too tired.

Elizabeth glanced at the stairs. She went up them on tiptoe, pushed open Gran's door, and looked in. The glow from the lamps in the room below showed her Gran's shape beneath a blanket, her head on a pillow. Grace was lying next to her. Elizabeth could see a liquid glint as the cat's eyes opened. She stood in the doorway a minute, then went back downstairs to extinguish the lamps.

The next morning, just as Elizabeth and Gran finished breakfast, Deirdre came to the door.

"Deirdre, I'm glad to see you," Gran said.

"I doubt that," Deirdre said rudely. She walked right over to the easel and stared at the painting resting on it.

"What's that supposed to be?" she asked.

"What you make of it," Gran replied. Deirdre shrugged, came to the table, and thrust out a note. Gran took it and read aloud, "Won't you both come for a sail with us in an hour or so?" It was signed Helen.

"Would you like to?" Gran asked Elizabeth. Deirdre marched off to a window. Grace drifted over to her. Deirdre began to bend, her hand reaching out to stroke the cat. Abruptly, she stood up straight and crossed her arms tightly across her chest.

"If you decide to come, don't bring food," Deirdre said. "Mama's making her usual horror picnic—wet cheese sandwiches and squashed tomatoes."

"Is Aaron going?" asked Elizabeth.

Deirdre looked at her with scorn. "You think they'd leave him alone? Maybe when he's fifty."

Gran began to wash the breakfast dishes.

"I'd like to come," Elizabeth said.

"Be down at the dock in an hour," snapped Deirdre, and left the cottage at a run.

"She wouldn't let herself pet Grace," Elizabeth observed.

"She's fighting a war."

"What war?"

"To show there is nothing in the world that pleases her," said Gran.

"Why?"

"I don't know why."

"Is it because they like Aaron so much more than her?"

"What makes you think that?" Gran asked sharply.

"They don't pay attention to her except to tell her to stop whatever she's doing and leave Aaron alone. But they're all over him."

"Is it your opinion that five pounds of attention equals five pounds of love?"

At Gran's words, a fire seemed to flare up inside Elizabeth's skull, burning her cheeks. "They sent me away when that baby was born!" she cried out. She sat down on a chair so hard it rocked.

"That baby," echoed Gran. She was drying a cup. After a moment, she spoke. "They did not send you away. They sent you to me," she said in a steely voice.

The hour, at the end of which she was to go to the Herkimer dock, was nearly up before Elizabeth spoke another word.

"Are you coming?" she asked.

She had been reading one of Gran's art magazines with desperation, trying to blot out a sense that her outburst had let loose some ungainly, mortifying thing that would now inhabit the cottage like a hobgoblin.

But Gran replied genially, as though nothing bad had happened, "Oh, no! I've always hated sailing . . . all that shouting—'coming about . . . hard to lee . . .' And you have to fling yourself from side to side so the boom won't decapitate you. Oh, no!"

"Well, I'll be going," Elizabeth said.

"Have a lovely time, my dear," Gran said with warmth. "I'll miss you."

By the time Elizabeth arrived at the dock, the Herkimers had gathered. On the top of Mrs. Herkimer's head rose a straw hat like a tepee. Several paper bags were at her feet. Aaron wore an orange life jacket, a sun hat, and long pants. Deirdre watched her father in the small sailboat as he bailed water that had collected in the cockpit with a rusty coffee can.

"This is a family tradition," Mrs. Herkimer announced to Elizabeth. "Every summer, we have our picnic at Little Bear Island. This will be Aaron's first time. Did you remember to bring the thermos, Deirdre?"

Deirdre, one arm around the mast, nodded.

"And I've made biscuits," said Mrs. Herkimer.

"For ballast," said Deirdre.

"Biscuits are traditional in our family," Mrs. Herkimer continued as though Deirdre hadn't spoken.

"'Over the sea in a pea-green boat . . .'" chanted Aaron.

"Ready. Let's go," called Mr. Herkimer. "Give me the picnic stuff. Where's the blanket? Deirdre, let go of the mast. Helen. You first, then Aaron, then Elizabeth."

A fresh wind plucked at the loose ends of the sail. As both Mr. and Mrs. Herkimer

reached for Aaron to lift him from the gangway, the boat swung wildly.

"No!" he wailed. "Let me get in by myself!"
But his protest was drowned out by his father
shouting that they wouldn't go at all if Aaron
was going to misbehave.

Though they were still anchored, their voices
were caught by the wind and flung out onto the
bay. Elizabeth felt a sudden excitement. She
was glad Gran hadn't come. She was glad the
Herkimers were so noisy and crazy.

The sail was let out. With a great smack, it
caught the wind. They were off.

"WHAT HAPPENED?" Gran asked as Elizabeth
burst through the door several hours later, her
hair in a tangle, her arms and neck sunburned.

"What a day!" cried Elizabeth. "Oh, those
soggy sandwiches! That oily lemonade! Mrs.

Herkimer talking about the glory of simple food. The tomatoes must have been sliced with a comb. When we got to this little island, it was rocks and a couple of runty pines and a tiny cove. Mr. Herkimer was mixed up about the tides, and he took this tremendous leap over the side and landed in about two inches of water.

"I thought he was supposed to be the quiet one in that family. He turned into the monster captain . . . he never stopped shouting orders—'Shift! Duck! Sit up!' And if Aaron wiggled his finger, they all started screaming at him. Just before we anchored at Little Bear, Aaron yelled, 'I'm getting off this horrible ship!' and they threw themselves at him so we nearly keeled over. When we got back, Mrs. Herkimer said she hoped I'd enjoyed a day of family sailing. Then Deirdre said, 'Don't thank her. It will only encourage her.'"

"I knew I had good reasons for staying home," Gran said, laughing.

"But in a way, it was wonderful," Elizabeth said. "I had a wonderful time."

"Life is strange."

"Like the Herkimers."

"I guess so. I'm going to make a cheese rarebit for supper, and while I'm doing that, I think you ought to write home. I noticed a pile of letters from your mother on the table."

Elizabeth glanced at them. They were filled with the astonishing news that Stephen Lindsay could hold his head up without wobbling, and that he really smiled.

She made a little space for herself at Gran's worktable among the brushes and pencils and tubes of paint.

She wrote briefly that she had gone for a sail with Gran's neighbors. Then, for the first time in a letter home, she mentioned Aaron. "He's a thin, little boy with eyes like a panda's. He says whatever he thinks." Elizabeth realized she was smiling as she wrote these words.

When she was finished, she looked up to see Gran watching her intently. Had she been looking at her all the time she was writing her letter? She turned her face away from Gran as though from too bright a light.

But Gran said, in a matter-of-fact voice, "Come to supper."

When Elizabeth had sat down, Gran held up her hands. "The weather's changing. I can feel it in my thumbs."

"I'm sorry I said that—in the morning— about being sent away," Elizabeth said.

"You said what you thought," Gran said.

The next morning, Elizabeth awoke to the sound of a heavy rain pounding on the roof. Gran had made a fire in the little hearth. The cottage felt deliciously warm and safe. Gran produced slickers for them to put on when they wanted to go to the outhouse.

After lunch, the rain stopped. By then, Elizabeth had made a start on *To Kill a Mocking-*

bird. It was a sleepy day. Gran worked on her drawing of *El Sueño*.

Toward the end of the afternoon, Elizabeth glanced at the windows.

"Look at the fog! You can't see outside," she said.

A few minutes later, she heard muffled voices. There was loud knocking on the door.

Gran went to open it. The Herkimers stood on the threshold, their faces glistening with moisture.

"Is Aaron here?" cried Mrs. Herkimer, looking frantically into the room.

"We can't find him," Mr. Herkimer said grimly.

Behind them, Elizabeth glimpsed Deirdre, her shoulders bent as though she'd been struck across them.

9

The Herkimers huddled together in the middle of the room, and the posts that had suggested trees or columns to Elizabeth now looked like the stout wooden bars of a cage. Fog swirled through the open door. Grace, her tail down, shot up the staircase.

"Has he been here?" Mrs. Herkimer's voice trembled as she asked this question, and her breathing was audible. She was not wearing her pearls. A loud crack came from the fireplace as a flame-weakened log snapped and fell among embers.

"I haven't seen him today," Elizabeth said. She wondered if anyone had heard her. The Herkimers continued to stare at her longingly, as though she could free them from fear.

"He wouldn't get lost," Gran said quietly. "He knows the island by this time."

"How can anything help in this fog!" cried Mrs. Herkimer. She grabbed Deirdre's shoulder and began to shake it. "You were supposed to watch him, you miserable girl!" she accused her.

"Stop it, Helen," Mr. Herkimer said, gathering his wife close to him.

"I was going to see him . . . but the weather . . . I was reading," Elizabeth said faintly.

Mrs. Herkimer covered her frightened face with her large hands. When she took them away, she appeared to have gained some composure. "It's no one's fault," she said.

"We'll all look for him," Gran said briskly.

"Not you, Cora," said Mr. Herkimer.

"But I will," Gran said without even glancing at him. "Get the flashlights, Elizabeth. The slickers, too."

He had wanted to be lost, Elizabeth remembered. Aaron, she cried silently. "We ought to try the cemetery first," she said. "We usually met there."

"The cemetery," Mrs. Herkimer repeated dully.

Gran kicked down the last log in the hearth, and it broke into a shower of sparks. "We'll leave a light burning to come home to," she said. She bent to turn up the wick in a kerosene lamp. Everyone watched her in silence.

As the wick caught and the chimney appeared to swell with the light, Deirdre said, "I'm scared."

Mr. Herkimer put his other arm around her. He looked at Gran. "You mustn't, Cora. I really wish you'd stay here. We'll be glad of Elizabeth's help."

"After we've done some searching, we'll report back to your house, John. I'll be fine.

One of you ought to stay at home in case he comes back."

"I'll stay," Helen Herkimer said. In a despairing voice, she added, "I'm the clumsy one, anyhow."

The Herkimers left.

"How can we find our way?" Elizabeth asked.

Gran hung a slicker over her shoulder and pressed a flashlight into her hand. "A step at a time," she said.

They went out of the cottage. "Look, it's thinning," Gran said. "You can see a bit of the sand spit."

They went over the slope to the meadow and up past the Herkimer house. It took a long time. They had to move slowly. Each step was like a deep-drawn breath.

It was only because they knew the way so well that their feet found paths their eyes couldn't see.

The fog was denser in low places. The light brush of grass against her legs, the hard roots in the ground beneath her feet, a sudden strong smell of balsam—these things comforted Elizabeth.

But her mind was filled with terrible images: Aaron dazed, wedged between rocks or clutching at seaweed and stones, trying to pull himself out of the bitter cold water, or wandering in circles in the woods.

The flashlight seemed to concentrate the fog, to turn it a sour yellow that blinded her. She turned it off. When she looked down at the ground, she was able to recognize the low, thorny bramble she knew was close to the barn.

"I'm going toward the ridge," Gran said. "You try the cemetery."

Elizabeth went on. Without the flashlight, she could spot a familiar clump of flowers, or a fallen bough, or a pile of stones that Aaron had gathered. A web of dampness covered her face and hands. At moments, she held out her arms in front of her, her fingers brushing tree trunks and low branches. She stumbled constantly on roots. It was like moving through a sack filled with wet cotton. She heard a distant foghorn lowing mournfully like an immense cow.

She came out of the woods. The fog was thinner. She looked up and saw a narrow stretch of starry sky. After a few more steps, it disappeared. She had to burrow like a mole into the long meadow.

Suddenly, her right knee hit a gravestone. She stood still. "Aaron," she called, as her fingers touched the grainy, rounded surface of the stone.

There was only silence. Were there ghosts? She wished there were. She felt so alone, so fog-chilled and helpless.

She went on. She heard waves breaking, withdrawing with their catch of pebbles and shells. She must be close to the farther end of Pring. There she could turn and go around the point and come back on the other shore. Then she remembered the great, black, jagged rocks.

The fog broke suddenly. She was on a point of land, looking at the ocean. The moon was nearly full. For a moment, she forgot why she was there. She looked at the water world, glinting, beautiful. The island was like a great ship. For a second, she had the illusion it was moving out to sea.

"Aaron!" she called urgently, again and again. There was no sound but the waves.

She went back past the cemetery. The fog still lingered in hollows like swaths of torn cloth. A low breeze sprang up. Soon, the Herkimer house loomed before her.

As she reached the screen door, Gran was walking slowly and heavily from around the barn. When she saw Elizabeth, she shook her head.

In the living room, the three Herkimers sat in a line on a sofa, each face like a pale, vacant mask. But as Gran and Elizabeth came in, they all stood up, and Mr. Herkimer bowed his head slightly as though this were some formal occasion. When he spoke, his voice was low, as though trying not to wake someone who had fallen asleep in some other part of the room.

"Our sailboat is gone. I've radioed the Coast Guard. There's a wind starting up and it'll blow the fog away, but it could blow a boat away, too. I'm sure Aaron took it. He always talked about sailing away. A boy's joke, I thought."

"The wind . . ." muttered Mrs. Herkimer.

"You can't be sure he took it," Gran said. She spoke with effort, as though out of breath.

"There was a coil of rope on the dock. Neatly done. The way I showed him how to do it," Mr. Herkimer said.

"You could have been careless, not tied up the boat properly. Anyone can make a mistake," Gran said.

"Go home, Cora. You must!" His voice rose, shockingly loud. "There's nothing we can do. The Coast Guard will find him . . . if the boat's afloat. . . ."

"It'll be all right," said Deirdre. "Daddy, you taught him what to do. You know he remembers everything."

Mrs. Herkimer began to cry soundlessly. Deirdre lifted herself onto her mother's lap. Her head covered most of Mrs. Herkimer's face, as though she could staunch her mother's tears with her mop of hair.

Gran stood. "We'll come back in a while," she said softly to Mr. Herkimer. He wasn't listening. She and Elizabeth went outside.

"We can't really be sure he took the boat," Gran said. "I want to keep looking."

"I'll go to the other side of the ridge," Elizabeth said. The fog was gone now, and she wasn't so afraid to chance the wild beach.

"And I have another place or two in mind," Gran said, her voice sounding faint.

Elizabeth shone the flashlight at her. She looked so old, her face collapsed as though the bones beneath her flesh had softened. "Go home," Elizabeth said. "Please! You look terrible."

"I can't bear to stop yet," Gran said. "I can't bear it. . . ."

They separated at the cottage. Elizabeth watched Gran walk past the dock and on toward the boulder where the cormorants came to dry their wings. She set out for the path up the ridge. At the top, the wind blew hard. But Elizabeth could hear the throb of an engine. Several hundred yards from the shore, a powerful searchlight cast its circle on the black water. It must be the Coast Guard boat.

She made her way down the ridge. The tide was high, the surface of rocks and stones wet. She struggled to keep above the waves that broke and foamed, gripping the roots and crooked branches of small trees, grabbing handfuls of sea grass, stepping on stones that rocked with her weight.

She passed above two coves, pools of moving darkness that absorbed at once the light of the flash she directed into them. She reached a farther cove just after passing the tidal pool where she and Aaron had watched the tiny, scurrying crabs.

Something bobbled, as a top does when it slows down. Before words could form in her mind, she knew it was the tip of a mast she had glimpsed below her. She shone the light.

The Herkimers' sailboat swung slowly from side to side, its bow caught between two rocks that rose from the water like canine teeth.

Tied to the mast by his shirt, his bare shoulders and chest luminous where moonlight touched, stood Aaron, his head fallen forward as though in sleep.

"I DIDN'T FIND HIM," Elizabeth said. "I just saw him before the Coast Guard did. They were almost as close to the boat as I was."

"He did the right thing," Mr. Herkimer was saying, "exactly as I taught him . . . he remembered what to do. . . ."

"You shouldn't have taught him to do anything," Mrs. Herkimer said accusingly. "It put ideas into his head, as we have seen."

"Anything puts ideas into your head," remarked Deirdre, carrying a tray of mugs of tea from the kitchen.

Aaron lay beneath a blanket on the sofa where, only a couple of hours earlier, his parents and sister had sat in dread. His hair was in damp spikes. He looked at the circle of faces of those who gathered around him. He seemed dazed.

"Elizabeth and I'll go now," Gran said.

"How can we ever thank you?" Mr. Herkimer said, and his voice was genuinely puzzled.

Mrs. Herkimer, her pearls restored, grabbed them up with one hand. "We would have found him by daylight—or the Coast Guard would have," Mrs. Herkimer said.

"Mother!" exclaimed Deirdre.

"I'm a realist," said Mrs. Herkimer. "I'm simply saying he would have been safe inside the cove. Of course, Elizabeth's finding him saved us a great deal of worry."

"Let's go home, Elizabeth," Gran said very quietly.

"Cora, you're worn out," Mr. Herkimer said. "I'll walk with you to the cottage."

"I'll be fine," Gran said. Then she added urgently, "I want to go home."

They started toward the door. "Elizabeth!" called Aaron.

She turned. Brother and sister were gazing after her. She saw how much alike they were— the same deep-set eyes and straight, dark eyebrows. Deirdre's expression was mild, even pensive. Aaron's mouth widened in a slow smile. At that moment, his face emitted a kind of radiance. Then he closed his eyes, and the light went out of his face.

The fog was entirely gone. The sky was cloudless. The moon in the pale dawn sky painted a
path across the water, which was already fading
away even as Elizabeth looked at it. Beside the
Herkimer dock, the sailboat, returned by the
Coast Guard, rocked gently.

"When Mrs. Herkimer thought Aaron was in
danger, she was almost nice," Elizabeth said.

"She's regained her usual self," Gran said.
"Back to a dose of self-congratulation every
twenty minutes."

When they entered the cottage, Gran walked
to the round table, where she sat down heavily
and lowered her head to rest on her hands.

"Gran?"

She sat up with effort. "It was wonderful
that you found him," she said. "Even if he was
safe in the cove, he was out of his head with
fear." Grace came to her and stood up with
her paws resting on Gran's knees. "Not now,
Grace," she said, and clumsily pushed the cat

away. "I miss plumbing at times like these. . . ." Her voice faltered.

Elizabeth went to her quickly and touched her hair.

"Are you sick? What can I do?"

"Help me upstairs. There's a chamber pot beneath my bed. Take it out. You'll have to go back to the Herkimers. Tell John to reach Jake. . . ." She said something indistinct. For a moment, her voice rose. "If he can't, he must call the Coast Guard again. I have to get to the hospital. I'm sorry, sorry. . . ."

Elizabeth's stomach seemed to sink, to fall out of her body. Her hands tingled and broke into a sweat as she helped Gran up. She kept her arm around her waist as they slowly ascended the stairs. In the small, bare room, she lowered Gran onto her bed.

"Blessed bed," she murmured.

Elizabeth stood irresolutely, afraid to leave, afraid to stay.

"Go now. Fast as you can." Gran's breathing was so uneven, Elizabeth had to guess at most of what she was saying. "I'll be all right. . . ." The last words were barely audible.

The dinosaur spine of the ridge flamed with the rays of the rising sun. The sky above was liquid with the rose light of morning.

She knocked only once on the door before John Herkimer, still dressed, looking exhausted, opened it to her.

"Gran," she uttered. A sob rose in her throat. "She's sick. She wants Jake to come and take her to the hospital."

Mr. Herkimer took her arm and drew her into the dining room. "It's too early to reach Jake. Anyhow, she'll need the Coast Guard. I'll radio them. You go and drink the tea I was about to have." He led her to the dining table, and she was grateful to be told what to do, where to go. He left her at once, running into the kitchen where he kept the radio.

"They're sending out a motor lifeboat," he told her when he returned a few minutes later. "They have some medical equipment, oxygen . . . she'll need that. And they're going to call the hospital in Ellsworth. She's got an emergency doctor there. Blystone."

Why would he know the doctor's name? Why hadn't he been surprised when she'd come to his door with such news?

He was looking at her closely, and he seemed to sense her confusion. "Your grand-mother didn't want to tell me but she had to, especially with you being here. I should have insisted she not search for Aaron with the rest of us. But when I found the sailboat was missing, everything flew out of my head. I couldn't think about anyone but Aaron."

"She didn't want to tell you what?"

"She's very sick," he said. "In the spring, she was in the hospital several weeks—"

"No one told me!" she cried.

He looked up at the ceiling nervously. They must all be asleep upstairs. For a second, she didn't care if she woke the whole household.

"I thought you ought to be told," John Herkimer said. "But she was fierce about that. She made me promise not even to tell Helen."

"Tell me what?"

"About her sickness. She has heart disease. She thought she could manage this month with you. She had to, she told me. She wanted you here."

Elizabeth got up from the table and ran from the room, Mr. Herkimer's words following her. "They'll be along soon—not more than forty-five minutes. . . ."

Grace was standing by the open door of the cottage, meowing for breakfast. Elizabeth went to the stairs and listened. There was no sound. Her heartbeats were loud in her ears. She quickly filled a bowl with dry food for the cat and went up to Gran's room.

She was asleep. Elizabeth looked down at her for what seemed a long time. Deep lines radiated from her mouth. Her hair looked dry, like doll's hair. Her breathing was labored, uneven.

She imagined Gran at the sink, smiling over her shoulder, her square, small hands in the soapy water washing a dish.

A framed picture Elizabeth had not seen before stood on the bedside table. It was of a very young man, his hair falling in curves along his cheeks, bound in the back with some kind of thong. He was smiling, looking down at something out of the picture. She recognized her young father.

She woke Gran.

"The Coast Guard is coming very soon," she said softly.

"I'll be ready." Gran's voice was somewhat stronger than earlier. "Help me downstairs."

There were fifteen steps. They paused on each one. Elizabeth took her to a chair and eased her into it.

"John told you?" she asked Elizabeth.

Elizabeth nodded.

"We—your parents and I—didn't know what to do. We talked for weeks. We wrote letters . . . whether to tell you or not. We'd be certain one day, then at sea the next. Somehow time passed. My doctor thought I'd be able to manage for a few weeks. And after all that talking and argument, life carried us along as it seems to do no matter what we choose. Last night's wandering around pushed me over the line. It was my own fault. I should have stayed here while the rest of you looked for Aaron. You found him anyhow."

Elizabeth heard the scrape of a bough against a window. The room suddenly brightened as light entered it like a spirit.

"Someone should have told me," she said. Was that right? Would she have wanted to know? Wasn't it awful enough to know now?

This minute? She put her hand across her eyes.

"Take your hand away, Elizabeth," Gran said. "You would have been watching me every second, the way the Herkimers watch Aaron, waiting for me to fall over. You would have been scared the livelong day. Maybe we were *all* wrong. But the way it has turned out—didn't we have good times?"

"You're going to die," Elizabeth said.

"Yes," Gran said. Her mouth twitched with the ghost of a grin. "Most people do," she said.

Elizabeth knelt beside her and covered her hands with her own.

"You must do something for me," Gran whispered. "You must tell the Herkimers to take Grace. I wouldn't want her abandoned again."

TWO YOUNG MEN in Coast Guard uniforms carried Gran on a stretcher to the Herkimer dock, where a sleek boat of forty or so feet was anchored.

Elizabeth followed, carrying her things, which she'd stuffed hastily into her suitcase and backpack. She had found the little metal giraffe Aaron had given her and, after a moment's hesitation, left it on a windowsill where it was possible to imagine it would look out across the bay all winter.

Mr. Herkimer had come to the cottage a little earlier to get Grace, and to press Gran's hand wordlessly as she lay on the stretcher.

A medical officer waited on the dock. "We'll make her comfortable," he told Elizabeth. "Then you can come aboard. There'll be an ambulance waiting in Molytown to take you to the hospital in Ellsworth."

She stood alone on the dock. The day was brightening around her. She recalled the first time she had seen Pring. It had seemed to her as flat as an old-fashioned postcard.

The officer called to her. "She's perked up a bit," he said. "You go and sit beside her."

Gran was lying on a cot that was firmly anchored to the floor by metal bars, in a cabin that resembled a hospital room. Two tubes led from Gran's nostrils to a cylinder of oxygen.

It was hard for Elizabeth to look at those tubes, and hard not to. Because of them, she guessed, two faint thumbprints of color touched Gran's cheeks. She seemed some other person, an old stranger drowsing.

Elizabeth sat down on a stool next to the cot and Gran opened her eyes. She reached out her hand. It faltered in midair and fell back on the coverlet. "So sorry . . ." she murmured.

"Don't be sorry anymore," Elizabeth whispered.

"You can call your father from the hospital," Gran said.

She was still taking care of things.

An engine rumbled. There was a sudden thrust forward as the boat moved away from the dock. "I'll be right back," Elizabeth told her.

From the deck, she gazed at Pring. Mr. Herkimer stood at the end of the dock, holding Grace. He saw Elizabeth and waved slowly. She lifted her hand once in farewell, and went back to the cabin. Gran had fallen asleep.

BECAUSE IT WAS so early and a Saturday morning, the roads the ambulance followed to Ellsworth were nearly empty. Gran seemed restless. She muttered, and constantly turned her head from side to side. Elizabeth felt she was losing her to a dim world where sentences were never finished, and where sleep came and went abruptly.

Dr. Blystone was waiting in the emergency room at the hospital. "We'll be putting her into intensive care," he said. "She'll need some tests."

A nurse directed Elizabeth to a small office near the reception area, where she found a telephone on a desk covered with framed photographs of someone's family. She looked at them as she dialed home. They all smiled at the camera; even the infant carried in the young woman's arms was smiling.

What were they really like? What were they smiling about?

Her father answered on the third ring. A radio was playing in the background. They must be in the kitchen getting breakfast. She heard a chuckle, a high, delighted laugh.

"Elizabeth! How marvelous to hear your voice! Listen—Stephen's talking to you."

"Daddy, I'm in the hospital in Ellsworth," she said.

There was silence at the other end of the line. She heard Daddy say, "Take him," and her mother cry anxiously, "What's the matter? Is there something—"

183

Daddy's voice came back on. "What happened?" he asked.

"Gran," Elizabeth said. "She's very sick. The Coast Guard had to come and get us. We're in the hospital in Ellsworth. They're going to take her to intensive care."

"I'll get the first plane to Bangor," her father said. "I'll rent a car at the airport. Oh, Elizabeth! We so hoped——"

Elizabeth interrupted him. "Please get here as fast as you can," she said. They both hung up.

She had heard the sounds of her home from which, after all, she had not been sent away like an unwanted package. She had had it all wrong, and Gran's assurances hadn't really changed what she had felt.

But she understood now. Maybe they should have told her, warned her about what could happen, what, in fact, had happened. The knowledge of Gran's illness would have altered the nature of those weeks in a way she could barely imagine.

But would that knowledge have lessened her shock at realizing Gran's weakness? Seeing those hard plastic tubes that brought her the life-sustaining oxygen? Perhaps she would have simply refused to go to the island if she had known. But then she would have missed everything. She was no more sure of what the right thing to have done was than Mom or Daddy or Gran had been.

Dr. Blystone came into the room. "You won't be able to visit your grandmother for a while," he said in a kindly way. "She's had a stroke, not the worst kind, but serious enough."

"My father's coming," she said.

"Good. You must be hungry. Go downstairs to the staff cafeteria and get yourself some breakfast. You couldn't have had much time for that."

She found the cafeteria, ordered toast and, for the first time in her life, a large container of coffee. Sitting down at a table with her tray, she recollected how she and Nancy had tried to stay up a whole night through but never managed it. She had now.

Mr. Benedict arrived just after noon. Elizabeth, by then, had spent five minutes visiting Gran. Her face was still. Elizabeth had bent close to her to hear her breathing. She'd spent the rest of the time in a waiting room, looking at tattered magazines without actually seeing anything in them.

When her father appeared at the entrance to the waiting room, she looked up at him. The magazines slid from her lap to the floor. For the first time since Gran had sent her to Mr. Herkimer to radio for help, she cried. Her father held her for a long time.

❧ 10 ❧

Elizabeth's grandmother died at the end of the third week in September.

On a Thursday afternoon, after dropping her schoolbag on the kitchen floor, Elizabeth lifted Stephen Lindsay from her mother's arms, sat down on a rocking chair, and held him upright on her lap. He regarded her seriously. She made a loud popping noise with her mouth. His lips trembled, widened into a smile. Then his voice rose in a cry of hilarity.

"I love to break him up," Elizabeth said to her mother, who was looking through a heap of catalogs that had arrived in the morning mail.

"I have no character," Mom said. "I hate these things, but I always look at them."

The wall telephone rang. Her mother went to answer it. "Charlie," she said. She listened. Elizabeth saw tears start from her eyes. Elizabeth clutched her brother to her, his breath on her neck.

After a while, her mother hung up the phone. She turned her wet face to Elizabeth.

"Gran is dead," Elizabeth said.

Stephen Lindsay let out a wail, and her mother took him. They stayed in the kitchen. Weeping, Mom poured a glass of milk for Elizabeth, put some cookies on a plate, warmed a bottle for the baby. There didn't seem to be anything to do but sit there thinking about Gran. Elizabeth wiped her eyes on a kitchen towel. She ate a cookie but tasted nothing.

After a while, Mom whispered, "I'll put Stephen in his crib now. I think he'll sleep."

On Sunday, the three of them flew to Bangor for Gran's funeral.

THE SERVICE WAS held in a Congregational church that had been built in 1853. The squeaking, high-backed pews that smelled of old varnish were nearly filled with people who had known Mrs. Benedict. On his father's lap, Stephen Lindsay fought sleep. The young minister who led the service tended to smile at odd moments, as though his thoughts and his mouth weren't quite in agreement. Perhaps, reflected Elizabeth, he was unsettled by her brother's occasionally loud chirps, which echoed high above the congregation like the sound of a trapped bird.

Yet, though he hadn't known Gran, the minister spoke of her in a tender way, the little smile coming and going, as though the simple fact that she had been born and had lived was reason enough for reverence.

Only a few people drove north to the Blue Hill peninsula for the burial where Gran had arranged, some years earlier, for a plot in a small, old cemetery on a hill.

The Benedicts made the trip in a rented car. Keeping steady speed in front of them was the hearse.

It was the first time they had all been together except for their hushed ride from Bangor, where Mr. Benedict had met Elizabeth, her mother, and the baby. He had spent most of the month in Ellsworth, with side trips to Camden and Pring Island when he could get away from the hospital. There had been many things to take care of, he told them, the accumulation of a lifetime, papers, paintings, other artwork of hers, furniture, and clothes, to be given away or stored. The cottage had been much easier than the Camden apartment.

"Did Gran talk a lot to you?" Elizabeth asked, feeling a certain shyness. Her voice sounded unnatural to her own ears. Was it because she was speaking of one so recently gone from life? *Gran* was now a word for a mysterious space. Yet in the part of her mind that flashed with ever-changing images, Gran moved among them, animated or at rest, sharp or kindly, as the mood took her. Elizabeth was, she realized, memorizing her.

"She hardly spoke," her father was saying. "She asked one time to see a picture of your brother. By the time I got it out of my wallet, she was drowsing."

Elizabeth glanced at Stephen Lindsay, asleep at last in his car seat beside her.

"That's all?" she asked.

He was silent for a few miles, his hands gripping the steering wheel.

"She worried so about a couple of envelopes she'd left in the cottage," he said at last. "One is for someone named Jake Holborn. The other is for you. They're back in that canvas bag on the floor. Even when I brought them to the hospital and showed them to her, she was so confused . . . didn't recognize them. It was terrible. She cried."

"Jake Holborn was the old man who brought supplies to us in his boat," Elizabeth said.

"Was he at the church?" Daddy asked.

"No," she replied. She drew two envelopes from the canvas bag, one printed in large letters with her name, the other with Jake's. She kept them on her lap.

After a time, her father said, "So many people came." Her mother drew closer to him.

They reached the narrow roads of the peninsula. A wind had risen. Dead leaves blew through the streets of the villages through which they drove. The houses were mostly shabby. Small grocery and hardware stores were closed and dark for Sunday, but everywhere, in yards, on front lawns, alongside cracked patches of sidewalk, old trees glowed, flaming with autumn color like festal torches, undimmed in the bright day.

Soon, a hill rose steeply in front of them. At the top, the hearse passed through the open gates of a white picket fence. Mr. Benedict parked behind several other cars on the grassy verge of the road.

"I hope Stephen won't wake when I pick him up," Elizabeth's mother said. "The wind's blowing so hard. Put that wool hat on him, will you, Charlie?"

Elizabeth, wanting to get away from her family, got out of the car, still holding the envelopes, and entered the gates.

The back doors of the hearse were open, and two men in dark suits stood beside them. Several yards away, an old man leaned on a shovel. Elizabeth saw a rectangular hole with clods of earth along its edges. She went quickly past it.

The cemetery must have covered four or five acres of the slope of the hill. Most of the gravestones looked older than the three on Pring Island.

There were people standing about, but Elizabeth kept her head down. Out of the corner of her eye, she glimpsed goldenrod and black-eyed Susans swaying wildly in the wind amid the tall grass that grew behind the fence stakes. When, past the last graves, the slope grew so steep she could go no farther, she looked up.

Before her lay a vast landscape. Over a long reach of water, a spidery green bridge arched to an island that appeared to be traveling into the eastern sky. Its shores were ringed with rocks and, here and there, a stone-strewn beach. A thin church steeple rose high above the roofs of a village. Everywhere, clusters of trees rippled and swayed in the wind, their red and orange and yellow leaves recalling to her the shimmer of a rug from North Africa, at home in the farmhouse, when sunlight touched it.

"Elizabeth!" a familiar voice called. Turning almost reluctantly, she saw Aaron. Behind him stood his parents, and Deirdre, astonishing to see dressed in a neat plaid skirt and blue blazer, her hair short and brushed. A few feet away, Jake Holborn lounged against the fence, his cap jammed down on his head, a wrinkled brown corduroy jacket hanging from his bony shoulders.

Aaron was staring at her uncertainly.

"It's me, Elizabeth," he said in a timid voice.

She had to speak to them. The older Herkimers murmured the words of consolation she had heard many times today. They were sorry, they said, that they had missed the service, but they'd had to pick up Jake in Molytown. Aaron touched her wrist briefly. "I wish she wasn't dead," he said.

Then Deirdre came close to her and pulled her away from the others.

"You were really lucky," she said in a low voice. "I told you that before. This time, I mean to have had someone like your gran who wasn't in the stew."

"Stew?" asked Elizabeth.

"The family stew," Deirdre said with her usual impatience, and left her side without another word.

Elizabeth took a few steps toward the Herkimers. "How is Grace?" she asked.

"Just fine," Mrs. Herkimer said. "We're extremely competent with animals."

"Naturally," muttered Deirdre.

"She's getting used to us, I think," said Mr. Herkimer.

"We must join the others," Mrs. Herkimer commanded as she took Aaron by the hand.

They moved away and Elizabeth went to Jake. "I have something for you, Mr. Holborn," she said. Jake nodded and straightened up. In one hand, he held an unlit, very stale-looking cigarette.

"I saw you just now looking down on Eggemoggin Reach," he said. "That's Deer Island across the bridge, where I used to live years ago before I went to Molytown. I'm really sorry about Cora Ruth. The Herks came all the way from Orono to pick me up. That was nice of them, but she did go on about her being so charitable all the way to here. I expect you know the way she is. Nobody ever needs to give her a compliment. Cora and I used to laugh about that. I see my name on that envelope so I guess it's for me."

Elizabeth handed it to him. He opened it, drew out a pasteboard with a drawing taped to it, and whistled softly. "I may just get this framed," he said.

The drawing of *El Sueño* with Jake standing in the bow rustled where the tape had come loose. He licked one finger and pressed down on it. "I'll fix it," he said. "That's a strong west wind. There'll be good weather for a time."

Elizabeth's father was motioning to her. As she climbed the slope toward the grave site, the gallery owner, the minister, the Herkimers, her parents, and a few elderly women began to form a circle. The coffin was suspended by ropes over the hole. She saw the minister's lips move, but his words were snatched away by the wind. The coffin was slowly lowered by the two men who had come with the hearse. Her father looked up at the sky, then let fall upon the coffin a handful of earth.

The grave digger continued to lean on his shovel, motionless as a statue. People stood around now, speaking in low voices. The gallery owner was making comic faces at Stephen Lindsay, who was fully awake and apparently trying to turn his head in a complete circle so he could see everything. One of the elderly women who was talking to Elizabeth's father, an earnest look on her face, suddenly burst into laughter. "So like Cora . . ." Elizabeth heard her say.

Aaron came up to her.

They stared at each other, then, as though they'd silently agreed on a plan, went a short way down the slope and sat on the ground near a small gravestone with an angel poised on top of it. One of its wings had crumbled away.

"That's your little brother?"

"Yes."

"Do you tell him what to do?"

"I can't tell him much of anything yet," Elizabeth said. She wasn't really paying attention to him.

Despite the wind, there was some warmth in the air, that late autumn warmth that makes you think of the hard, cold months to come.

She stretched her legs out in front of her. The mystery of the land and sea spread out beyond the hill—it seemed like the whole earth— filled her with wordless anticipation.

Gran had said you can't pursue happiness. It can strike in the middle of trouble, and it can disappear for no apparent reason, even when you think you ought to be happy.

"What's in that envelope?" Aaron's question interrupted her thoughts.

She opened it and drew out a sheaf of drawings. Every one of them was of her.

"Look!" Aaron said excitedly. "That's you washing dishes. Here you're reading with your hair falling all over your face! Your shoe's off and it's under the table. Here's one of just your back. There's Grace on your lap. I love Grace. She doesn't say anything. Look at this one! You're asleep in the chair. What were you stirring in the bowl?"

No one would ever see her exactly as Gran had seen her. A great shaft of loss went through her.

"Maybe you were making cookies for me," Aaron said with a touch of slyness.

Elizabeth turned to look at him. She examined his face closely, his straight black eyebrows, his dark eyes, his large ears, the spiky hair. He began to smile.

"You remembered me!" he said.